THE HOGBOON
OF HELL

Nancy and W. Towrie Cutt

The Hogboon of Hell

and other
Strange Orkney Tales

Illustrated by Richard Kennedy

ANDRE DEUTSCH

For ERNEST W. MARWICK,
Benefactor and lover of Orkney,
A true and never-failing friend

First published 1979 by
André Deutsch Limited
105 Great Russell Street London WC1

Printed in Great Britain by
Cox & Wyman Ltd
London, Fakenham and Reading

British Library Cataloguing in Publication Data

Cutt, Margaret Nancy
   The hogboon of hell, and other strange
   Orkney tales.
   1. Tales, Scottish – Orkney Islands
   I. Title   II. Cutt, William Towrie
   398.2'1'0941132   PZ8.1

   ISBN 0–233–97020–7

Contents

ECHOES OF THE SAGAS

Acknowledgements

In compiling this collection of tales taken from or inspired by Orkney folklore, the authors referred to the following publications and would like to acknowledge their debt: Walter Traill Dennison's *Orkney Folklore and Traditions* (Edited with an Introduction by Ernest W. Marwick, published by the Herald Press, Kirkwall, 1961) and *The Orcadian Sketch Book* (published by William Peace and Son, Kirkwall, 1880); Ernest W. Marwick's *The Folklore of Orkney and Shetland*, with excellent bibliography, (published by Batsford in 1975); Hugh Marwick's *The Orkney Norn* (published by Oxford University Press in 1929); Mary A. Scott's *Island Saga* (published by Alex P. Reid and Son, Aberdeen, in 1967).

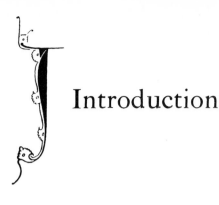

Introduction

The least known folk-tales of the British Isles may well be those of Orkney. In these long-inhabited isles, however, where the farm house jostles the site of stone-age burial mound or Pictish broch, and the majority of place names speak of Norse saga and history, there is a wealth of traditional lore. Tales of the ritual of scissors and sieve, of the sinister and indestructible Black Book, of the seal ancestor and of the witch raising up the storm at sea, were told in Orkney homes within this century. One of the writers of this book heard his grandmother recount the story here entitled 'St Magnus for Orkney' in substantially the same form that it was known to the Tudor historian, Holinshed. Around 1880, Walter Traill Dennison, the Sanday scholar, set down a number of old tales that he had heard in island cottages. Five of these – 'The Stolen Winding Sheet', 'Johnie Croy of Volyar and the Mermaid', 'Annie Norn and the Fin Folk', 'Eyn-Hallow Free', and 'A Close Tongue Keeps a Safe Head' – are included here. Their lively dialect, strong in elements of the original Old Norse, is no longer widely understood, so the tales have been retold, but with as few changes as possible.

Other stories, 'The Blue Cow from the Sea' and 'Grammarye, Fog and Fire', among them, have been expanded from very brief originals. Every attempt has been made to keep them in general agreement with Orkney folklore and legend.

A third group, for example 'The Storm Child', 'Sworn on

the Odin Stone' and 'The Hogboon of Hell' is largely imagined. Each tale has, however, arisen from some undeveloped point of interest in Orkney tradition or folklore – the names of the cottages, Paradise, Hell and Purgatory, for instance, or the legend that the Standing Stones can move. Some are variations of well-known tales. 'Rest in Peace' is an attempt to fill a gap: there being no known tale of a woman *returning* from Finfolkaheem, one has been invented.

Although Orkney has few ghost stories, 'The Stolen Winding Sheet' challenges Scotland's best. Tales of witches and Spae-Wives abound. Orkney giants and fairies are not represented, being on the whole rather inept specimens of their kind. The Orkney Trow (descendent of the Norse Troll) appears as a Hogboon. We must look in vain for larger-than-life heroes and grand heroic conflict in these fireside tales of an essentially practical people, fishermen and farmers.

There is nonetheless much colour and romance in the tales testifying to the domination of the sea over island life. In it dwelt mysterious and marvellous folk, the sea horses and sea cattle, and the terrifying demon, the Nucklevee; from it emerged in human form the friendly Selkie, the sinister Fin Man and the lovely Mermaid. The seal body of the Selkie harboured a human soul, either that of a drowned person or of an early Odin worshipper awaiting Judgment Day in this form. Fin Man and Mermaid were of supernatural origin: lesser angels these, long ago rejected by Heaven and Hell alike for their refusal to choose between God and Satan during the War in Heaven. Having occupied Earth, they fled again from the coming of man, taking refuge in water, mountains, caves and forests. Twilight and the return of the seasons, Yule, Johnsmas, All Hallows', released these resentful spirits briefly into man's world to entrap human souls and win the Devil's favour. Especially dangerous was their attendance upon the hours of birth and death, when they were only driven off by protective ritual and symbol, by candle-lit wake, the

Spae-Wife's spell, the carrying of salt or iron or steel. The sign of the Cross and Christian prayer were, of course, all powerful against them, but from 'Eyn-Hallow Free' and similar tales and legends, it seems that the prudent Orcadian added, in the interests of safety, some of the old spells and charms.

In such mixtures of homely practicality and vivid imagination lies much of the interest and vitality of Orkney's folklore.

APPARITION
AND GRAMARYE

Nine Stones Wake

1. *Wee Herd*

At three o'clock in the afternoon, Maggie Matches followed the cows from Biglands along the road to the hill pasture. Spotted Flecko, black-and-white Backie, and five or six others with no special names walked sedately in line. Old Onmark, a red cow with a stupid white face and one crooked horn, lagged behind and after Onmark, dragging her feet, dangled Maggie, who was wee herd for the rest of the week. The 'piece' that Mrs Duthie had given her – oatcake and cheese – shared her pocket with the pebbles that she had gathered in the morning. She had left her knitting behind on purpose. Maggie was in a bad temper.

Mrs Duthie had scolded her earlier for throwing stones at the gulls in the ebb.

'Shame on you!' said Mrs Duthie. 'You might as well be a tinker boy with no one to tell you better. Throwing stones! A big girl of nine . . .!'

'I *will* throw stones!' said Maggie aloud, remembering. She took aim. 'Stupid cows!'

The pebble hit old Onmark, who switched her tail and hurried to join the others. Maggie's temper still simmered, and the stony lump in her throat refused to be swallowed down. She kicked a tussock: it hid a stone.

'I'll run away!' said Maggie, hopping on one foot and trying to hold her hurt toes. She knew she was being silly – where could she run?

Behind her lay Benjie Breck's farm, Biglands; these were Benjie's cows. The tall stone house of Biglands faced the road, its byres, sheds and barns forming a hollow square behind it. Nowhere to run there. Maggie and the cows had just come out of the back gate into a narrow road where they walked now between low stone dykes. People who left Biglands by the front gate and turned left on the road passed the school and the school-house. Turning right, they came to the manse and the kirk. The graveyard went along the side and around the back of the kirk, and had another gate on the road. A little farther along were three cottages; across the road, the bakehouse, another cottage, and the sheds for the pier.

Maggie lived in the cottage next the pier. From its door a few steps took her to the low stone jetty where her father's lobster boat, the *Whaup* tied up. It was not there today; her father had gone before she woke up.

She wished she was back on the beach there now with its brown barnacled rocks. When the tide ebbed, it left rock pools and jellyfish and lumps and tangles of weed where the birds fed and squabbled. Across the road, the fields behind the bakehouse ended at more rocks and sand. On every side, the sea, grey or blue, met the sky. . . .

Nowhere to run, thought Maggie angrily. They all see everything I do. Minding cows . . . !

The cows turned into the pasture through a gap in the dyke marked by an upright slab of grey stone as tall as Maggie. They scattered and began to graze. Cattle from the other farms were not there this week. Maggie was the only herd on the hill.

Not far away the Trows' Howe jutted up steeply like a grassy castle with two tall stones standing near the top. They were called the Watchmen. A little brown drystone wall ran up one side of the Howe, across the top and down the other side, so that no careless beast should fall into the quarry. Maggie could see into the quarry and she knew how deep it was. The manse and kirk, Biglands House, the school and school-house, and the cottages too, were all

made of its stone, as well as most of the walls dividing the fields. Children were not supposed to climb the Howe to look over the wall at the top into the quarry, but they always did.

'Keep the cows away from the Howe,' said Benjie Breck that morning.

'As if I didn't know!' muttered Maggie now. In the morning, under Mrs Duthie's disapproving eye, she had said nothing.

'Don't go near the quarry,' said her mother anxiously when Maggie left the house. Maggie had not answered; she had heard this warning all her life.

'I *will* climb the Howe!' she said. 'And I'll look over the wall! And I'll whistle, too!'

Benjie Breck, who was Superintendent of the Sunday School, had rebuked her on Sunday for whistling near the kirk.

'Maggie! The Lord's Day! No whistling! And this is the Lord's house! No whistling by it at any time. Your mother would skelp you if she knew!'

'She would not!' said Maggie aloud now. 'You can't stop me now, Benjie Breck!'

Avoiding a bed of nettles waving in the wind near the foot of the Howe, she began to climb. Half-way up the steep slope, edges of rock showed grey through the grass. Almost at the top, the two great upright stones, the Watchmen, leaned towards each other across the grass and nettles like people talking. They were nearly three times as tall as Maggie herself.

A peewit arose and cried ahead. Maggie flung a pebble and missed. 'I hope it broke your eggs,' she said nastily. And she stepped hard on the scurrying burying-beetle that came out from under a stone.

'I'll – I'll not go home,' said Maggie. 'Not while *he*'s there!'

But she knew she would. Where else could she go?

'I won't be his wee nurse!' she said, gritting her teeth. 'He can take care of himself!'

He had arrived in the night while Maggie slept. In the morning, there he was. Mrs Duthie was moving about in the kitchen instead of Maggie's mother. *She* was in bed, and too sick to say much except,

'You must help Mrs Duthie, Maggie,' and 'Don't climb the Howe!' when Maggie was leaving.

The cradle that had been Maggie's stood near the fireplace. Under the edge of a woolly cover showed the top of a little round head with a red wrinkled face in front and a tangle of black hair behind. It was awake when Maggie got up; it had howled itself to sleep while she ate her porridge. Black-and-white Gow, who was called Maggie's dog, sat looking down into the cradle, his head cocked, his one black ear raised, listening to the little sobs and snuffles that came from under the blanket after the baby went to sleep.

'Gow!' Maggie had said crossly. Gow wagged his tail and stayed by the cradle. When the baby sighed he cocked his head the other way and raised his white ear, panting a little.

'Gow!' But Gow did not move.

'More peats, Maggie!' said Mrs Duthie. 'You'll have to help your mother a bit more now. She's been very sick.'

'It's all *his* fault!' said Maggie, scowling at the cradle.

'Now, now!' said Mrs Duthie. 'He's your brother, and goodness knows they've waited long enough for him. He's a bonny baby, too,' she added, looking down into the crib. 'Bigger than you – such a trowie wee thing you were, sickly and . . .'

Maggie stopped listening for several sentences. I'll just *be* trowie, she thought, as useless as . . .

'Peats, Maggie!' said Mrs Duthie loudly, turning oatcakes on the girdle. Maggie went out, dragging her feet. At the door, she collided with fat Nellie Borwick from the bakehouse.

'Eh, Maggie what's this I hear? It's grand your mother has a wee nurse for the baby. Have you been tending him yet?'

'No!' said Maggie sourly. She detoured around fat Nellie and went to the peat stack. Returning with her load, she was in time to hear Mrs Duthie.

'. . . an ill-bisted little thing today! If you said water was wet, Maggie would say it was dry!'

'Maggie'll have to draw her claws in now,' said Nellie with a fat chuckle. 'Would you rather Dr Sabiston brought you a sister in his bag?' she asked, as Maggie set the peats on the fire.

'No!' snapped Maggie. 'And there's only bottles and scissors and things in that bag,' she added.

Mrs Duthie clucked her tongue and shook her head. Nellie only laughed.

'As if I didn't *know*!' thought Maggie.

'Well, James will be glad he has a son to go in the *Whaup* with him – here's Dr Sabiston now!'

A long shadow fell across the floor.

'How are my patients?' asked the doctor. He was tall and thin, and Maggie liked him better than she did most grown-ups. But today she liked no one and it seemed that nobody liked her.

'She's asleep, doctor,' said Mrs Duthie.

'I'll look in,' said the doctor, setting down his bag. It clinked like bottles and scissors, and Maggie looked at Nellie, but she did not seem to have listened. He glanced into the cradle as he passed.

'This one's doing well,' he said. 'On guard, old fellow?' he asked Gow, who stood up politely and wagged his tail. The doctor went on into the bedroom, Maggie and Gow at his heels.

'Stay here, Maggie,' said Mrs Duthie sharply, and Maggie turned back. The lump in her throat hardened as Gow padded back to stop by the cradle.

'She'll do,' said the doctor, coming back into the kitchen. 'Where's James?'

'Off to the lobsters,' answered Mrs Duthie. 'I told him he could stay at the hut – I don't want him under my feet for these first two or three days.'

'*He*'ll be well satisfied with what you brought in your bag,' said Nellie.

'And how about Maggie?' asked Dr Sabiston kindly.

'Put him back in your bag – *if you can* – and take him away!' said Maggie. '*I* don't want him!'

The doctor burst out laughing and picked up the clinking bag. 'No, no! Maggie. Your father and mother wouldn't like it. You'll just have to make the best of him!'

Still laughing, he went out, and Maggie heard him speaking outside to Benjie Breck. She did not like Benjie, the big, red-nosed farmer from Biglands, who was, in some queer way, a kind of cousin of her parents. She disliked his loud voice and his wheezy laugh and the way he ordered the children about if he saw them loitering in the road. He always called her 'Wee Maggie', and sometimes he scolded her.

As Dr Sabiston drove away, Benjie marched into the kitchen, filling up the doorway cutting off the square of early sunshine on the floor.

'Good-day, Mrs Duthie! Good-day, Nellie!' he boomed.

Both women hissed at him to speak softly. 'Well, Wee Maggie,' he went on in a hoarse whisper, 'You'll have to be a proper sister to this lad. Your father will soon have a boy for crew in the *Whaup*.'

Maggie said nothing, glowering at him under her thick fringe.

Mrs Duthie shook her head and glanced at Nellie.

'Now, Maggie,' said Benjie, puffing a little, 'I must have a wee herd for the cows in the afternoon for a day or two. Kitty Corsie's wanted at the house then, but she'll be morning herd and keep the cows off the road and out of the turnips and away from the other cattle. The boys are all singling turnips – there's no' another child in the village to be had, and I spoke to your father this morning before he left. You can take the cows at three o'clock.'

'I don't want to be wee herd,' said Maggie sulkily.

'Shame on you!' said Mrs Duthie. 'And your mother sick and all.'

Benjie paid no attention to either of them.

'Now if Wee Jamie was a few years older, I'd ask him,' he said wheezily, and laughed. 'But he's over-young – so we'll just make do with Wee Maggie. Keep the cows away from the Howe,' he added, 'and stay away from the quarry.'

Maggie said nothing. Benjie turned to the women.

'Maggie's wee,' he added, 'but she's active. She can take her dog and the time will pass.'

He glanced at the cradle, and Gow raised both his ears.

'Will her mother need her?'

'No, no,' said Mrs Duthie. 'I'm here till James comes back, and a day or two more. Dr Sabiston didn't want her left alone with the children. She'll do well enough, but she's still weak.'

Five minutes later they had settled that Maggie would be wee herd for the next few days. She was to watch the cows from three o'clock till eight, and get her supper at Biglands and threepence a day. Mrs Duthie would give her a 'piece' for the afternoons.

'I don't know what to make of you, Maggie, and that's a fact,' said Mrs Duthie after Benjie had puffed out. 'You spend all day up the hill with Kitty Corsie and the cows whenever you get the chance – and now you say you don't want to go. And Benjie paying you threepence . . .'

Maggie stopped listening. But no matter how she sulked, here she was – wee herd for nine cows in the hill pasture – and climbing the Trows' Howe.

'Nobody asked me if I wanted to go,' she thought angrily as she picked her way around more nettles. She was half-way to the top and she looked down at the cows. They were grazing peacefully, old Onmark quite near the foot of the mound. Maggie scrambled a few yards higher on the steep slope, and looked the other way over the fields. Far off, a line of boys and men moved slowly across a field, singling turnips. She could see over into Biglands too – it all looked small. A cart and horse stood near the byres.

Somebody – Benjie perhaps – came out of the house and went across to the byre.

Maggie gritted her teeth.

'I'll whistle if I want!' she said. 'I'll whistle on the road, and I'll whistle on the Howe, and I'll whistle by the kirk too!'

Puckering up her drooping mouth, she whistled shrilly, once and again.

2 'Wha Whistled?'

'What whistled?' said a slow, grating voice to the left. Maggie spun around. No one was there.

'Blo-o-ow!' moaned another to the right.

'*I* whistled!' said the wee herd loudly, looking from one to the other of the tall stones in search of the boys she was sure must be hiding behind them. 'I whistle when I please.'

And she whistled again, scrambling the last few steps up to one of the Watchmen and throwing a pebble at the other. No boy was hiding there. The nettles stood up straight and tall all around them. No one could have been there. But who had spoken?

The shadows of the Watchmen, like her own, fell away to the north-east; they were still quite short. It was a long time until eight o'clock and supper. Gulls wheeled overhead. A rabbit watched nervously from behind a grey boulder. Maggie felt suddenly uncomfortable and wished for Gow. Then she remembered that he was probably still sitting by the cradle and was angry again.

'*He's* taken my dog!' she said.

She threw another pebble at the farther Watchman, took a long look over the low wall down into the quarry, and started back down the slope of the Trows' Howe.

A little cracking noise came from behind. Startled, Maggie turned just in time to dodge a stone the size of an apple rolling down the slope straight at her.

'Who threw that?' she shrilled indignantly, turning

towards the Watchman on the right. A shower of earth and pebbles tumbled down the slope behind her from the left, and another lump rolled to her feet. Maggie kicked it, and it fell away into dust and sand. Only a little thin stone with two or three dark spots on one side lay there.

'Blo-o-ow!' groaned a voice from the right.

'Whustle!' grated the other from the left.

'I'll whistle when I please!' snapped the wee herd. She threw her last pebble at the Watchmen, and picked up the little slim stone, intending to throw it too. It was lighter than she expected, light as a dried leaf. Its hollow ends were packed with earth, and when she poked at it, a long thin core of hard clay fell out. A little greenish stone whistle or pipe lay in her hand. It was about the size of a man's thumb but thinner, one end smooth, the other jagged as if part of it had been broken off. Three little holes in one side were still plugged with clay.

'A whistle!' said the wee herd, forgetting to be angry. She blew gently into the smooth end, and her breath came out in a queer long moan that lasted long after she stopped blowing. All the cows raised their heads and looked at her. More earth and pebbles rolled down the slope, and Maggie moved down two paces.

'Nine Sto-o-ones wa-a-ake!' moaned a voice from above her.

'Wa-a-ake soo-o-on!' came the other like an echo.

'Stones don't sleep!' said the wee herd rudely and blew a toot on the whistle. The sound went on and on.

'Sto-o-ones wa-a-ake!' droned the voice. Maggie thought it came from the Watchman she had hit with the pebble.

'Wa-a-ake!' echoed the other.

'Then wake!' snapped Maggie. '*I* don't care!' And she blew two sharp toots to prove that she didn't. They sounded so odd that she took the whistle from her lips and looked at it. It seemed heavier than before. One of the holes had cleared itself and she poked out the others. Another shower of earth and pebbles came flying. Maggie jerked away, shutting her eyes just in time as a sharp pebble hit her on the nose. Then she slipped and tumbled down the rest of the slope, clutching the whistle tightly.

When she scrambled to her feet at the edge of the nettle bed, Old Onmark stood almost at her elbow and the rest of the cows were moving up, all staring at her.

'Mind your own business!' said Maggie angrily. 'Be off with you and eat grass!' She stamped her foot and put the whistle in her pocket. Onmark switched her tail and turned about, setting off for the farm. The other cows hurried to fall into line behind her.

'Stupid cows!' cried Maggie, rubbing a dock-leaf on the nettle burns on her hands and arms. 'It's too early – it's not eight o'clock!'

The cows, now some yards away, slackened pace at once, scattered and began to graze. Maggie drew a deep breath. She took out the whistle, looked it over carefully, weighed it in her hand, raised it to her lips, took it away, and finally blew very very softly into it. It moaned sadly – a long, long moan.

'Stones wake?' she said quietly. 'They do not! What stones are asleep?'

'Tro-o-oll sto-o-ones . . .' muttered the wall near by. Jerking around in alarm, Maggie picked out an ugly-looking solid grey chunk as the speaker.

'Nine . . . wa-a-ake . . .' grated the turf somewhere under her feet. Maggie jumped aside.

'. . . soo-oo-on,' finished the muttering voice in the wall and an echo came from up on the Howe.

Everything fell silent.

They talk when I whistle, thought Maggie Matches, feeling very important as well as frightened.

'Be quiet now!' she said to the stones. Not one answered back, and she felt safer. Suddenly she was hungry.

Only the day before she had sat with Kitty Corsie on the wall here, eating her piece. Today the wall was different. It talked, she thought uncomfortably. Perhaps it doesn't *like* to be sat on? Suppose a stony arm came out and

grabbed . . .! Or the wall threw me down and fell on me . . .! What did it say – *troll stone*?

She was afraid to blow the whistle and ask.

'Be quiet . . .' said the wee herd shakily. She put the whistle in her pocket, turned her back on the Howe and the Watchmen and the talking stones, and hurried after the cows. A couple of them were lying down, beginning to chew the cud. Maggie sat down near spotted Flecko and ate her piece, chewing every bite carefully to make it last. She no longer felt like throwing pebbles. Rabbits came out and nibbled near by, and she sat still, feeling the whistle in her pocket. It was light, light as a feather, smooth and cold. It just fitted her little hand.

They speak when *I* whistle, she thought, feeling important. And she smoothed the little stone pipe. But somehow she did not blow it again, even walking back to the farm at eight o'clock. It might disturb the cows, she told herself. Someone might take it away.

'It's *mine*,' said Maggie aloud. 'No one knows about it.'

The cows turned in the back gate of Biglands and went to the byre. Benjie Breck came out of the house.

'Well, Wee Maggie – how did you pass the time with no one to talk to?'

'I spoke to the cows and – and the stones!' said Maggie boldly. Benjie laughed, as she knew he would. Silly old thing! she thought. He doesn't know what I know!

'Aye . . . aye . . . and they answered?'

'Yes, they did!' said Maggie cheekily. Benjie felt in his pocket.

'Here's yer threepence, lassie. There's supper for ye in the kitchen. Three o'clock tomorrow – and ye can gab away to the stones!'

'I'll show him!' thought Maggie.

In the kitchen, the wee herd ate her supper in silence. Annie, Benjie's housekeeper, was no talker, and Kitty Corsie had already gone home. A few minutes later, Maggie turned out of the front gate and started down the road, the whistle clutched in her hand, light as a dried leaf. Past the kirk, where Benjie had said, 'No whistling at any time.'

There's stone, thought Maggie. No one was in sight. She raised the whistle to her lips and breathed gently into it, awakening its sad moan.

'Ha! Ha! Benjie Breck!' she said aloud.

Not even an echo came back from the kirkyard wall, but near the gate something rumbled creakily. A gatepost?

One that talks, said Maggie to herself and slapped the gatepost cheekily as she passed into the kirkyard. Turning her back to the manse in case anyone was looking, she blew the whistle. No sound came. Harder – the whistle was dumb. And blow as she might, all remained silent save for the twitter of the starlings. The gravestones were all silent: anything they had to say was carved on them. 'Born 1821, Died 1847', or 'Here lies Elizabeth Lennie' – things like that.

'You're afraid to speak!' said Maggie scornfully. 'I'm not afraid to whistle! I *will* whistle!'

But she had to pucker up her mouth to do it, for the little green stone pipe was quite dead. She blew it again as she went out of the gate, and just as she passed the wall the end of her breath came out strangely. Again something muttered – not the gatepost as she had thought, but the long grey flagstone under her feet. She felt it vibrate and jumped to one side. Gow, coming to meet her, howled dismally and dashed off to the cottage, tail tucked under.

Again Maggie was afraid. She put the whistle back in her pocket and ran down the road after the dog.

'What did you do to the dog, Maggie?' asked Mrs Duthie crossly. 'Did you throw a stone at *him*?'

'NO!' said Maggie, looking indignantly at Gow who stood between her and the cradle, shivering a little. 'I wouldn't hurt him!'

Her mother was awake and asked about Maggie's afternoon. There was not much to tell, except for the whistle, and Maggie was not going to mention that. They'd take it away, she thought, and keep it for *him*. It's mine!

The baby was asleep; when he woke up and cried, Mrs Duthie fussed over him and took him in to his mother and stayed there, talking. Maggie, left alone, called to Gow, but he would not come. When she went to him, he lifted his lip ever so little, and growled, ever so softly.

'Tell-tale!' said Maggie. 'See if I care!'

She fondled the whistle, light and cool, and *magic*.

Tomorrow I'll blow it in different places, she said to herself. I'll see what it does. I'll make those stones talk, and find the others – they said *nine* . . . No one else can do that.

Feeling important, she went to bed and put the whistle under her pillow. No one should see it; no one should blow it but Maggie. Clutched in her hand, it stayed cold, even when she held it for a long time. Still holding it, she went to sleep and dreamed . . .

The Watchmen were coming down the Howe, across the field. Tall and grey and dreadful, they moved slowly, swinging from side to side, first one edge, then the other advancing. They moved in a straight line – they fell on anything in the way and crushed it and got up all in a stiff piece and came on – straight – straight towards Maggie and the whistle that she couldn't stop blowing . . .

Maggie cried out and woke and sat up. She was in her bed and Gow was growling in the kitchen. Someone – Mrs Duthie, her mother, perhaps – spoke to him. Maggie lay down and went to sleep.

3. 'Sto-o-ones Gro-o-ow'

In the morning the whistle was under the bed, and Maggie had almost forgotten her dream. She thought of the talking stones while she dressed. Four in the pasture – two Watchmen, Left and Right. Lacing her boots, she wondered what they would say today. I won't let them say much, she decided, they have such ugly voices and they made me fall into the nettles. Number Three – one ugly grey squarish stone in the wall . . . And now she was scared to sit on the wall! That stone had said *Troll stones* – must find out about that! One stone – Number Four – that grumbled under the turf at the foot of the Howe. She was not afraid of that one, she would make it talk – what could she ask it? And how could she keep the others from hearing the whistle?

'Breakfast, Maggie!' said Mrs Duthie. 'Did you wash?'

Maggie hadn't, so she did. While she ate her porridge, she thought.

The flagstone at the kirkyard gate made five. And why was the whistle silent in the kirkyard? It couldn't be because of Benjie. She would try it again. And how could she find four other talking stones?

'If only I could whistle where I please!' said Maggie. But whatever happened around the cottages was seen. Children threw stones or quarrelled – and were seen or heard. Everybody knew who washed windows or shook rugs or wore a new hat. It was hopeless at home, too. Mrs Duthie kept her busy all morning.

'Sweep the floor, Maggie. You'll have to get used to helping a bit more now.'

'More peats, Maggie! Do wake up!'

And 'Run over to the bakehouse, Maggie, and ask Nellie for a loaf and six flour scones and four currant.'

The bakehouse was even worse,

'I hear there's a fine wee laddie at your house, Maggie,' said old Mr Borwick, the baker, coming out of the back with his floury apron and the peel in his hand. He looked at her over his glasses; he wore them down his nose because of the steam.

Maggie said nothing, ducking her head and frowning.

'Eh, your father's pleased wi' his boy,' said Mr Borwick and went back to the oven.

'How *is* the baby this morning, Maggie?' asked Nellie.

'I didn't see him,' said Maggie coldly. It was quite true – she had refused to look at him when Mrs Duthie called her over. He was horribly disappointing – all red and helpless

and howling. She had expected him to be pink and cuddly and playful – and bigger – other people's babies were.

'And your mother?' persisted Nellie.

'She's all right,' said Maggie, scraping her foot along the side of the counter. Nellie gave her a sharp glance – almost as if she had seen her mother's disappointed look when Maggie turned her back.

'Eh, well . . . !' said Nellie wisely. 'Tell her I'll be in to see Wee Jamie later. Here . . .'

She handed over the bread and scones, all warm from the oven and smelling very good.

Maggie put them in her basket. As she stepped out of the bakehouse door she looked both ways. Nobody in sight! Whipping out the whistle, she blew very softly. Hardly any sound came out, but somewhere down the pier a stone rumbled in reply.

Six! said Maggie.

The gull sitting on the capstan screeched and flew, and a dozen starlings lined up on the roadside dyke suddenly whirled shrieking into the air.

'Mercy! What's gone wi' the birds?' said Mrs Duthie, coming to the door. 'It must be a hawk after the hens.' And she looked anxiously towards her own chicken coops next door.

Maggie knew better. First the cows, she thought, then Gow, now the starlings. They don't like the whistle – but it makes them *do* something. Six talking stones! I'm the only one who knows!

She decided to test the whistle later, along the road and in the pasture and find the other three stones. There was something else about it too – the way it felt, sometimes light, sometimes heavy . . .

Back in the kitchen, Gow lay at the bedroom door, or by the cradle.

'Watching his lamb!' said Mrs Duthie.

'He used to watch Maggie like that,' said Mrs Matches.

He doesn't like me any more, thought Maggie. For very quietly, as if he didn't want the others to know, Gow warned Maggie off, bristling his neck, showing his teeth if she came near. At three o'clock he refused to go with her.

'Then *stay*!' said Maggie. '*I* don't want you!'

And she left without saying goodbye to her mother, and took her piece – currant scone with jam – without saying thank you to Mrs Duthie.

'Take no notice of her,' said Mrs Duthie at the bedroom door as Maggie went out. 'She'll come round – she'll have to make the best of it.'

Maggie did not wait to hear her mother's reply. She loitered at Biglands until the cows were out of the gate and well ahead of her.

'Be off with you, Maggie!' said Benjie as he trundled across to the sheds.

Maggie made a face at his broad back and blew the whistle just as she went through the back gate. Behind her, a clatter broke out in the horse-barn. Willie Duthie shouted and swore, and Benjie hustled out of the shed to see what was wrong.

'Ha! Ha! Benjie Breck!' said Maggie aloud. 'All that fuss for a little whistle! And that's seven!'

The taller of the two tall slabs that formed the gateposts had moaned. The cows had turned around, stopped, and bunched behind old Onmark, who tossed her head and snorted.

'Hush!' said Maggie crossly. 'They'll hear!'

But the echo of the whistle lingered, dying away very slowly. Maggie hurried after the cows. They quieted when she spoke, and moved on in line after the echo died away. Maggie decided that Number Seven, awake or asleep, had better be left alone – it was too near the farm. Someone would find out.

She left the cows grazing just inside the gap, and hurried off to scramble half-way up the Trows' Howe. The whistle, light as a snowflake in her hand sounded shrill and clear, the notes hanging in the air long after the whistle was back in her pocket. While the sound lasted, the stones answered to it, the Watchmen first.

'Sto-o-ones gro-o-ow!' said the one on the left.

'Gro-o-ow!' echoed his mate.

'. . . o-o-ow!' came from the foot of the Howe.

'*Grow*?' gasped Maggie. 'Stones can't grow!'

'Blo-o-ow!' ordered the left hand Watchman, and 'Blo-o-ow!' moaned the right.

'No! I won't!' said Maggie aloud, gripping the whistle in her pocket. It grew strangely heavy as she spoke. Did it want to be blown? Maggie turned and hurried down the Howe, moving across the slope at an angle, for it was too steep to run straight down. Again she stumbled, again earth and stones came flying at her, again she tumbled the last few feet.

'I won't whistle for you if you do that!' said Maggie angrily. '*Grow*, indeed! Whoever heard of stones growing?'

But she gave the stones no chance to answer. The whistle stayed in her pocket for the next two hours and everything was quiet. Maggie ate her piece and even felt a little sorry that she had not been pleasant to her mother. She thought the baby might improve after he had grown a bit. Grown . . .

Then she began wondering what the stones meant when *they* said 'Gro-o-ow'. If the Watchmen grew, how would they do it? Grow larger – or grow arms and legs? Both ideas were horrid.

Fidgeting with the whistle in her pocket, she decided to find out what the stones at the foot of the Howe had really said. She had not heard them clearly. I'll stay well away from them, she thought. I'll blow very softly so the Watchmen won't hear.

The whistle was pleasantly cool to the touch, light as a feather when she raised it. She barely breathed into it and the air was full of whispers at once when,

'Blo-o-ow!' muttered the grey stone. 'Nine Gr-o-ow!'

Maggie blew softly again. 'Grow?' she whispered. 'What stones grow?'

'Tro-o-oll sto-o-ones gro-o-ow!'

A sudden sharp crack sounded from the wall. Several of

the small flat stones above the big grey one fell to the ground. The turf rumbled at the foot and she jumped back. A crack was opening between a pink-tipped daisy and a dandelion – it opened and widened until it was two or three inches across. Maggie stared in horror. *It grew* she thought – it must have grown!

'Blo-o-ow!' It was like an echo all around her. 'Blo-o-ow' from above her. The Watchmen had heard her after all. The whistle was still light.

'No!' said Maggie, and the whistle grew heavy. I should throw it away, she thought. It's dangerous – maybe I will.

She went away towards the cows and stayed with them until she saw Kitty Corsie wave her apron at eight o'clock. By then Maggie had decided to keep the whistle, but not to blow it, or not often. She would be very careful. The stones would mind her – she would find all nine, and make them tell her about growing and waking. She would ask the flat ones – they couldn't do much harm. The one at the kirkyard gate . . .

The kitchen at Biglands was hot and smelt of new bread. There was thick soup for her supper and bannock and cheese and a sweet bun. Maggie ate rapidly.

'Maggie wants to get home to the baby,' said Kitty Corsie who was still there.

'No,' said Maggie, 'I want –'

'To see the baby!' mocked Kitty, laughing. Maggie knew then that everybody had heard that she was jealous of the baby. The last of the bun stuck in her throat, and she slipped off the bench.

'Goodbye,' she said. 'Thank you for supper.'

And she ran down to the road. The whistle had been light for some time, but it got heavy when she neared the kirkyard gate.

'It wants to be blown,' said Maggie, forgetting that she meant to be very careful. No one was near. She blew a tiny little toot. Under her feet the flagstone grated and groaned.

'-o-ow'. 'Blow'? Or 'Grow'?

Maggie found herself inside the gate. Again she blew and blew. The whistle was light as a snowflake now and quite silent. It doesn't like the graveyard, thought Maggie, and blew once more, just as she went out of the gate. The sound hung in the air outside the kirkyard.

'Gro-o-ow!' The starlings whirled up with shrill cries and there was a sharp crack. Maggie was flung forward on hands and knees on the edge of the road. The long flagstone in the path had split across just at the line of the wall.

Maggie scrambled to her feet and ran home.

'Look at the knees of your stockings!' said Mrs Duthie.

'I fell,' said Maggie.

Nellie Borwick and one or two other women came in that evening to visit her mother. No one took much notice of Maggie, who went to bed early. Lying there with the whistle in her hand, she thought how surprised they would be if she blew it, and made some stones speak. This was better than remembering what really happened when the stones spoke. They were so – so rough. Twice they had made her fall down the Howe into the nettles, and showered her with earth and pebbles. Now she had been thrown down at the kirkyard gate. What next? She felt cross with the whistle.

I just won't blow it outside again, she said to herself. I'll keep it safe – no one shall know.

She pushed it under her pillow and went to sleep to the sound of friendly voices laughing in the kitchen. . . .

It was a dreadful dream. She was outside, and she blew the whistle. It did not stop sounding when she took it from her lips. A cold wind blew; she was as cold as ice. And the whistle whistled all by itself. A great cloud was climbing up the northern sky, stopping, changing shape, coming on and up, closer and closer. The freezing wind blew off it. It changed colour – now pale and misty, now grey and solid looking – like stone. Icy gusts whipped up the grey peaked waves higher and higher. The cloud changed shape too – it stood in peaks like mountains and then rounded into a great head with a face of mist, looking down. Thunder rumbled far off, then close and loud, and mingled with the rumble of stones coming to life. The wind moaned like the whistle . . .

Maggie awoke. Moonlight lay across the floor, and the bed covers had slipped off. Gow whined softly at the door. She got up and looked out of the window. The sky was clear, the bay shone under the moon. Maggie seized the whistle – it was icy cold. She put it in the drawer of the chest.

'You can stay there!' she said.

Gow padded away into his corner and lay down. Maggie made her bed, said last week's Bible verses, and went to sleep.

4. Making the Best of It

Maggie remembered the dream when she got up. She stole a look out of the window. In the sunlight, things looked as usual, and she forgot that she had been frightened. The whistle lay quietly in the drawer; she thought she would do without it today. It would be dull in the pasture with only the cows there . . .

Mrs Duthie complained that she had not slept well. The dog had fussed all night.

'It's outside for you tonight!' she said to Gow who dropped his head and looked ashamed. 'Set the table, Maggie, and see if your mother is awake.'

Mrs Matches was awake. She hadn't slept well either. Jamie woke up and howled, and Mrs Duthie said something about washing clothes and giving Maggie's room a turn-out. It was a tiresome morning.

'Feed the hens, Maggie, and look for eggs.'

'Weed that flower-bed, Maggie.'

'Mind – be careful – don't break that . . .'

When Maggie left at three o'clock, she took her knitting. She took the whistle, too. Not to blow, of course – but Mrs Duthie might be putting something in the drawers. It was safer with Maggie – just to look at – and think about . . . *About what to do with it.*

This was not easy. The whistle went heavy. It dragged on her pocket when she knitted. It seemed to coax her fingers towards it when she put her hand in her pocket. She had done this so often in the last two days that it had become a habit. Like holding the whistle – like blowing the whistle.

The cows trailed off obediently along the pasture road. The back gatepost had no chance to say 'Wa-a-ake!' or 'Blo-o-ow!' or 'Gro-o-ow!' as Maggie passed by it, knitting, even though the whistle dragged at her pocket.

She sat down not far from the wall and the crack that had come in the turf the day before. It was still there; Maggie kept an eye on it. It did not open further.

The farm cart came out of the back gate and rattled cheerfully along the road towards her. Benjie Breck was driving.

'What does *he* want?' said Maggie crossly, and felt the whistle grow heavier.

If I blow it, she thought, the horse will run, or kick. Benjie wouldn't know I did it – he'd never guess I whistled . . .

She laid down the knitting and grasped the whistle, cool, smooth, lighter now.

Benjie brought the cart through the gap and along into the floor of the quarry. There he began loading stone, occasionally prying or hammering. For a while there was only the sound of his tapping and the scrape or thud of stones being loaded. Maggie moved closer to the quarry side of the Howe, staying at the low end of the wall at the foot of the mound. The whistle was in her hand – she raised it.

'I won't *really* blow it,' she said, 'just a tiny little whistle . . .' And she breathed into it. The air filled with whispers at once.

'Wa-a-ake!'

'Blo-o-ow!'

'Ni-i-ine sto-o-ones . . .'

'Gro-o-ow!'

Or was it 'Go-o-o'? A low muttering came from under-ground.

The horse was snorting and pricking his ears. Benjie spoke to him, holding the bridle. The whispering echoes went on and on.

'Nine sto-o-ones go-o-o . . .' moaned the square grey one in the wall.

'It did say *go*,' thought Maggie. 'Not *grow*!'

Benjie could not have seen her on her side of the wall. The depth of the quarry cut him off from the slope of the Howe. The grey stone in the wall moved, jerked, fell out of its place scattering smaller stones, and rolled over towards Maggie.

'Blo-o-ow!' it said threateningly. 'Ni-i-ine sto-o-ones go-o-o!'

The crack in the turf was widening. Maggie ran around the end of the wall towards the floor of the quarry.

The Watchmen! she thought. The Watchmen! Did they hear? Are they moving?

She looked up. Something grey moved at the edge of the drop, the top of the Howe.

Maggie screamed and waved her arms.

Benjie, still trying to control the horse, saw her and took two steps towards her. The horse jerked ahead. And a big grey boulder that Maggie could not remember seeing before crashed down where the horse and cart and Benjie had been a moment before.

'It moved!' gasped Maggie. She could hardly speak. The whistle dragged at her hand – she thrust it into her pocket. The whispering was dying away; Benjie seemed not to have heard it.

Benjie stood looking at the stone. His cheeks were mottled but his big nose remained as red as ever. He drew out a large blue-spotted handkerchief and wiped his face.

'You're a sharp wee lass, Maggie,' he said 'I'm no' just

ready to join the kirkyard congregation yet awhile. Did
you see it move?'

'Yes,' said Maggie. 'Up there . . .'

Her arm wobbled as she pointed.

'Umf . . .' said Benjie. 'I wonder why it fell?' He kicked
the sullen grey lump.

Maggie said nothing. That's Number Eight – I made it
move, she thought. I didn't know it would do that. She did
not feel clever or important – just frightened.

'A bad one,' said Benjie, jabbing the boulder with his
crowbar, and turning back to the horse and cart. 'Time the
quarry was closed off. The edge is crumbling.'

He loaded a few more pieces of the flat stone he had been
prying off, and went back to the farm. Maggie sat down
and ate her piece. Her hands shook when she tried to
knit.

The stones said 'go', she thought. They moved. Where
will they go? It's all the whistle's fault . . .

But she knew who blew the whistle – the troll's
whistle . . .

At eight o'clock she plodded back to the farm. The whistle
seemed to know that she would not blow it. It lay quietly,
neither light nor heavy, even when she passed Number
Seven at the back gate and Number Five at the kirkyard.
Once in her room, she put it back in her drawer and began
to think about it.

I must hide it, she told herself, hide it where no one will
ever find it. But where? If I put it in a rabbit hole, it would
soon turn up again. The well? But they clean it out every
year. I'll have to throw it into the sea.

She took it out of the drawer and looked at it. It was a
pretty little thing – the stone was greener and shinier than
she remembered, and smoother. It just fitted her hand . . .
Before she realized it, she had raised it to her lips and begun
to breathe into it. She caught her breath back again and
the whistle uttered two queer little hoots.

It said 'Ha! Ha!' thought Maggie, clenching her hand

around it. It was light, light and smooth and cool. She looked around nervously lest she had awakened a stone – awakened Number Nine. Out in the next room the hearth-stone and the mantel, the window sills, the lintels – all seemed quiet.

'Bedtime, Maggie,' said Mrs Duthie. 'Did Benjie say if he wanted you tomorrow?'

'He didn't say,' replied Maggie.

'Well – he'll let us know in the morning. Now off to bed.'

Maggie went quietly, still holding the whistle in her pocket. Maybe in the house the whistle had no power – as in the kirkyard. (But it *had* said 'Ha! Ha!') If she kept it at home and hid it carefully she could still take it out once in a while and find Number Nine and make it talk – if it was a *safe* one, of course. She could wake it, whistle to make it speak, maybe let it grow – but never, never let it move.

'Go-o-o!' they had said. Where would they go? Number Eight had gone into the quarry and tried to kill Benjie and the horse, Maggie was almost sure of that. They could only go if the whistle was sounding.

Absently, Maggie had raised the whistle to her lips. A little breath passed into it – it moaned, stopping as she jerked it away in fright. The sound echoed mournfully between the walls . . . it lasted . . . Gow howled. There was a grating, cracking from the next room. Number Nine! Awake – moving!

Maggie ran out of her door to see the heavy stone mantel-shelf lift and tilt from one end. The tall, shining brass candlestick tottered at the edge, ready to fall. Mrs Duthie at the other door screamed, but she was stout and moved slowly.

Maggie ran across to the hearth, caught the end of the heavy cradle and pulled. It slid slowly, then faster, and the candlestick crashed down, hit the foot of the cradle and rolled away across the floor. Wee Jamie began to shriek.

Maggie scrambled to her feet, dashed out of the door and across the road to the pier. The whistle seemed to weight her down, her steps slowed. She got there breathless and held on to the capstan.

'Blo-o-ow!' came a hollow murmur from the stone in the pier.

It's awake! thought Maggie – it's Number Six and it's awake. I wakened them all – the Troll stones – all nine. If I blow, they'll grow – they'll move!

She clutched the whistle, heavier than it had ever been. The sea! I'll throw it in the sea!

But she could not take it from her pocket.

'Blo-o-ow!' grated the invisible Number Six. 'Sto-o-ones go-o-o!'

'I can't!' gasped Maggie, and found that she could. The whistle had grown lighter. She pulled it from her pocket, raised it to her lips – light as a snowflake and as cold, smooth, magic – and *bad*.

Maggie caught her breath, shut her eyes and banged the troll whistle down as hard as she could on the rim of the iron capstan beside her. It shattered into splinters. A sharp piece gashed her forehead and a cold thrill ran up her arm, far far worse than if she had cracked her elbow. The pier shook and rumbled under her feet.

Maggie sat down hard, crying as if her heart would break. Her face smarted where the stone splinter had cut it, but her arm was beginning to feel warm again and she could move it. A wet tongue licked her cheek, and Gow whimpered and pushed her with his cold nose. Maggie put her arms around his neck and cried into his rough hair.

The pier was quiet, but lights were lit at the cottages and people were talking loudly.

'Maggie, Maggie!' called Mrs Duthie. She did not sound cross. Gow barked, but Maggie sat there, too tired to move. Willie Duthie came and picked her up and carried her home.

'Why did you run away, Maggie?' said Mrs Duthie. 'Look – Wee Jamie's safe – you pulled him away in time.'

There was a big scar on the end of the cradle where the

candlestick had dinted the wood. The mantelshelf was still tilted a little; dust and mortar lay on it, and a crack ran up between the chimney stones.

Maggie's mother was drinking hot milk with something in it from a bottle.

'You too!' said Mrs Duthie, cup in hand.

'It's nasty!' protested Maggie. Mrs Duthie put in a large spoonful of treacle, and Maggie drank it.

'Me too!' said Willie Duthie.

'You'll get nothing out of James Matches' bottle from me,' said his mother. 'Be off with you!'

Willie went out, laughing. Maggie went to bed and slept. Gow lay by her bed whimpering a little in his dreams. But for Maggie there was no dream and no whistle.

In the morning, the *Whaup* was tied up at the jetty. Her father stood out in the road talking to the minister and Benjie Breck.

'Mr Firth thinks it was a little earthquake,' he said when he came in. 'The flagstone's heaved and cracked at the kirkyard gate.'

'Aye,' said Benjie. 'A tre-more.'

He looked at the mantelpiece and at the cradle and shook his head. 'A tre-more . . . Maybe more than one . . . James, the quarry's crumbling. Wee Maggie warned me of a stone falling yesterday.'

Kitty Corsie came in with a message for Benjie.

'I'll take the baby home, Mrs Matches,' she said. 'We'd like a baby. I hear Maggie doesn't want him.'

'NO!' said Maggie. 'He's mine – I like him now.'

Kitty went out laughing.

Dr Sabiston came in. 'What's this I hear about candlesticks?' he asked. 'Maggie, do you still want me to take Jamie away?'

'No!' said Maggie. 'I'm keeping him. He's mine.'

I saved him from the stone, she thought. But she didn't feel clever or important – only glad. She looked at him and wondered how she was going to make the best of him. He did look much nicer today – pink instead of red, and he had tiny little soft hands.

The farm cart rattled along, and Benjie Breck went out, still talking about 'tre-mores'.

I saved *him* from the stones, too, thought Maggie, even if I did whistle to start them falling . . . *He's mine too!* What am I going to do with him?

But she remembered in time that Benjie didn't know much about it, and drew a sigh of relief. I'll just have to make the best of him too, she decided.

M.N.C.

Sworn on the Odin Stone

It was the last day of October. Ragged wisps of cloud drove across the darkening sky, and the woman in the cottage doorway shivered in the chill gusts. Her companion broke off to say impatiently,

'Get thee within, Mary! I'll come tomorrow for an answer. And think well, lass. A heathen oath on the Stone of Odin should not bind a Christian soul.'

He turned away, a bearded man of about forty, roughly but warmly dressed. Glancing down the road leading to the Bridge of Brodgar, he shook his head. There below, well apart from the ring of standing stones, the great holed Stone of Odin stood by itself near the bridge.

Behind him, the woman at the door was looking apprehensively in the same direction. The moon was rising, veiled by scurrying clouds; the roar of the sea came faintly on the gusts. Then she went in as bidden, barring the cottage door against the wild night, but unable to shut out the chill that came over her when she remembered the Odin Stone oath. The hand that had clasped hers through the hole in the stone was long cold in death: there could be no retraction now . . .

The dim light of the crusie lamp showed her to be about twenty-five or six, thin and poorly-dressed. Her fair, anxious face softened momentarily into its earlier prettiness as she looked at the box-bed where her children lay. She drew the blanket up over them, and sat down in a straw-backed chair by the hearth to knit. But her troubled glance turned often to the bed, and several times she rose to comfort and soothe the child who coughed and moaned in his sleep.

The fire burned low after a couple of hours, but she dared not replenish it from her scanty store of peat. Drawing the shawl closer around her, she took down a thick old-fashioned Bible from the shelf and opened it on the table beside her. Between the pages lay a folded letter. She spread it out, smoothing the stained, ragged page, and read again, by the dim yellow light, words that she knew by heart. Hastily and crookedly written, they were crowded into the last two inches of the sheet below the careful cramped signature.

. . . Mary, remember our oath on the Odin Stone to marry none other. I would come back from the dead for my bairns if you wed a man like him my mother wed. I am going up the country next week . . .

But he had never returned from that journey. Five years ago the swift cold waters of a northern river had claimed him. And because he had been but a short time in the service of the Hudson Bay Company, very little money had come to his widow, Mary Tait of Treb near the Bridge of Brodgar.

Tonight, utterly weary, listening for the sick child, and watching the warm glow of the peat fall into grey ash, Mary Tait spoke aloud.

'Aye, Andrew, my lad, I've missed you sore as you missed me. And I remember our oath on the Stone never to wed another. Oh, I remember, Andrew, and it has cost us dear . . .!'

She laid down the letter and gave the sick child a drink.

'And now that oath stands between your bairns and the good food and the warm house that Walter Clouston offers us. Walter that was ever your friend. Would ye hold me to it now, Andrew Tait? I would ye saw us three this night!'

With a heavy sigh she sat down again, folded the letter and shut it back in the Bible. Then she picked up the coarse knitting. But her hands dropped, and she nodded and dozed to the sound of rising wind. Unheeded, the crusie flickered out. The peat ash was long cold.

Some time later she awoke with a start. The gasp died in her throat. Inside and out all was silent, but the door was wide open. Black against the moonlight stood a figure that she knew, even in its unfamiliar garb of *capote* and moccasins.

Struggling to rise, she was powerless; no sound came when she tried to speak. Silently the dark form advanced to the table, silently opened the Bible and took out the stained letter. He spread it without a rustle, and, dark as it was in the room, seemed to scan the page by the faint, eerie light that emanated from him, yet left his features in darkness. Then he laid it down, open, on the Bible, smoothed it gently as she had done, and turned away. As he passed the box-bed, the sick child tossed and murmured. Without a sign he passed out into the night and behind him, untouched, the cottage door closed silently.

Only then did Mary Tait hear again the sound of the wind. Recovering the use of her chilled limbs, she crossed the room to try the door. It was barred as she had left it. Drawing the blanket up over the children, she lay down by them, and was instantly asleep.

She was awakened early in the morning by a heavy knocking. Pale and heavy-eyed, she admitted Walter Clouston.

'What do you say, Mary? My door is open to you and the bairns if you will but say the word.'

He paused. 'I – I dreamed of Andrew last night . . . I cannot think he would mind, Mary . . .'

'I saw him,' whispered the woman. 'He came – he stood there by the table – he looked at his letter . . .'

She realized that the paper still lay open on the Bible. But when she picked it up, the letter ended with Andrew Tait's signature two inches from the bottom. All reference to the promise made on the Stone of Odin had vanished.

'I will speak to the minister this morning,' said Walter Clouston.

M.N.C.

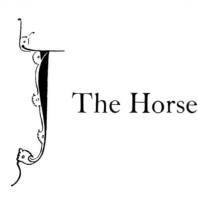

The Horse

The annual meeting of the free kirk had come to an end. Doctor Windwick and his wife walked back the short distance to their house, which was also his surgery. He was in a black mood.

As treasurer, he had reported that the kirk was five pounds short of meeting the minister's salary, and he had urged that all put an extra threepenny bit in the plate next Sunday, and suggested that the children could help by putting in a penny or halfpenny of their sweet money. But John Muir, a tight-fisted, well-to-do crofter, had risen to say he was giving all he could, and it would not hurt the big farmers, the doctor, and the schoolmaster to give a pound each. The children clapped their hands. As Windwick was giving generously of both time and money, he was annoyed; but two farmers rose and offered a pound, and then another, and the doctor and schoolmaster had to do the same. That is why he went home in a black mood on a black and windy night.

The maid, Maggie Jean, met him at the door to say that Davie Marwick had called over an hour ago. He wanted the doctor to come quickly, for his young wife Jessie expected the baby any minute. The time was eleven-thirty. With bitter thoughts of kirk folks, mothers, and babies, Windwick took the lantern from Maggie Jean, went to the stable, and harnessed the horse. As the maid had lit the candles in the gig lamps, he was soon on his way, his little collie dog, who always went with him, bounding ahead gleefully in the wind.

The pony was young and spirited, a dun half-blood with long pasterns. Having been idle all day, he tried to break into a gallop, to catch the dog ahead, but his driver held him to the trot. Between the last few houses of the village they clipped, and out on the lonely plain of Fidge, the high gig rattling over the metalled road. This plain stretched for two miles north, links lying to each side. No houses or fences bordered the road, which ran between rabbit warrens and sand hills. But the telegraph poles marked it, and one after another flashed past. The doctor having to hold his pony to the trot, his temper did not get better.

About half-way across the plain, near an old shattered post that had stood there a long time, the horse suddenly stopped with a snort and almost sent Windwick out of his gig on the road. Snorting again, the pony reared up, trying to turn round first to the right and then to the left, but the doctor held him. The little collie bounded into the gig, crouched to its master's feet, and lay there shaking and whimpering. Then the man became aware that his hair stood on end; he felt it push against his ears. But he held hard. Forward the horse would not go.

A faint sound came to Windwick's ears, and as it neared it became louder, sounding like the thuds of a horse's hooves over the links on the left. The pony had his head turned to the sound, his eyes glaring, his ears like bugles. Two clip-clops sounded on the road just in front of the pony, and then the thud of hooves on the links to the right. The sounds died as with a sigh.

Dog and pony stopped trembling. The hairs on the doctor's head lay down, and at his word the pony sped north over the plain, the dog six yards ahead. Soon they came to the bay on which a big farm stood, and beyond, the cottage of Davie Marwick. The doctor tied the horse to the gatepost, told the dog to lie in the gig, and entered. Davie showed him to the bedroom in which his young wife lay, her mother sitting by her side. 'Jessie's easier now, Doctor,'

said the mother. 'I thought the bairn would be born two hours ago.'

Jessie was looking up wanly. Windwick asked her a few questions, felt her pulse, and examined her. Then he told the mother that it might be another two hours, and asked her to have plenty of hot water ready. Davie then conducted the doctor to the parlour where Jessie's grandmother was sitting, small, pale, and wrinkled, a smile on her face that might mean welcome or amusement.

'Weel, Doctor,' she chuckled softly, 'you'll have had a tiring day of it.'

'Not very, Mrs Moodie, except for the kirk meeting tonight. I nearly resigned my job as treasurer. Folks want a kirk, but give little, and give it grudgingly.'

'Aye, aye,' she chortled. 'They think the minister gets plenty for his two hours on Sunday. This would have been the annual meeting.'

'Yes, it should have been earlier. The last day of January is late to clew up the business of last year.'

'The last day of January, is it?' She looked up, her pale blue eyes wide. 'Met you with anything strange on Fidge, Doctor?'

He started. 'Why do you ask?'

'Weel, you would not be the first. Both Jimmie Skea and Geordie Sinclair have had the wits scared out of them on this very date, and weel I ken why. But heard you anything?'

'Why, yes, and not only me. My pony stopped dead, and shook like a reed in the wind, and my dog cowered to my feet. Then came the sound of horse's feet on the links.'

'Aye, that's it. You heard the horse.'

'The horse! What horse?'

'Andrew Elphinstone's horse. This happened when I was little more than a bairn. Andrew of Copness was a hard man on his servants and tenants, and a hard drinker, drinking himself to destruction. He often came galloping home from the ale-house at night, lashing his grey horse to a lather. He was found dead on the first day of February, half-way across Fidge, near that old splintered post. His horse dead, too, a good bit away from him.'

'Dead. He broke his neck, I suppose.'

'No. His clothes were burned off him, and his horse, poor beast, its hair charred, lying about a furlong away.'

'Struck by lightning?'

'Aye, that's why the post is splintered.'

'But it is not on the road.'

'It was until they straightened out the road and put metal on it. A man long ago tried to make a farm out of the links, but could not make a living. That post is all that is left of his cot and fence.'

'Wasn't the horse killed with Andrew? Why was it that far from him?'

'Folks thought it went galloping round in a circle, its hairs burning till it dropped dead.'

'Well, Mrs Moodie, that explains my ghostly encounter. Only one would think that Andrew would haunt the place. Not the horse.'

'Hee, hee, hee,' she cackled. 'He's roasting in hell for his sins. The lightning ended his cursing and drinking. But, Doctor,' and the old voice whimpered, 'I pity that horse. Not yet at rest, poor beast!'

W.T.C.

By Scissors and Sieve

Mrs Brough and her stepson Johnny brought home the last load of their harvest in the darkness of a Hallowe'en night. The horse was tired, Johnny and his stepmother were tired. The old cart creaked noisily. The harvest had been wet, causing them much extra work. When they came to the stack yard, Mrs Brough went to the house while Johnny unhitched and stabled the horse.

She found that Jessie, a lass of nearly fifteen, had a muckle supper ready – a harvest home feast. The puddings, made of oatmeal and suet stuffed into the intestines of a sheep, had boiled for three hours, and were ready for the table. Home-brewed ale stood ready for the pouring. Mrs Brough laved her hands and face in a basin of warm water. Johnny came in, and he, too, laved his hands and face, first spitting in the basin.

'What are you doing that for?' asked his sister in disgust.

'So stepmither and I don't fight,' he sputtered, drying his face.

'A silly and dirty old habit,' cried Jessie. 'All our lives we have never quarrelled with stepmither.'

'Weel, bairns, may it always be like that. Johnny wants to make sure.' She had noticed a coy look on Jessie's face when she came in, and had thought it was because the supper was all ready. Now she noted a red knot tied in the girl's hair, but was too tired to give it a thought. Hungry as a boy working all day in the field can be, Johnny sat down and began eating, the other two soon after. When they had finished, Johnny and Mrs Brough sat in straw-backed chairs, one at each side of the fire, while Jessie cleared things away. The two talked of how much bere and oats they would be able to sell, and if a beast or two would be ready for market, and if they would get enough money to buy a new plough for Johnny.

'I tell you, Stepmither, that we must have it. That old wooden thing will fly apart the first stone I hit.'

'Yes, you need it, Johnny, but we must have the money.'

So they talked of the days ahead, and neither noticed that Jessie had slipped out into the darkness. But they did note her return. The door burst open and banged shut. Jessie sat down with a dump on a chair, a peeved look on her face. The noise she made brought a reproof from her brother.

'Can't you shut the door quietly?' he growled. 'Stepmither and I have had a hard day of it. Why? What's that red thing in your hair for?'

'Never you mind, brother.'

Mrs Brough suddenly remembered it was Hallowe'en.

'Whom did you see, Jessie? Was it the one you expected?'

'I saw nobody,' she answered sulkily.

'Did you whirl the scissors in the sieve ninety-nine times?'

'What on earth are you two talking about?' demanded Johnny.

'It's Hallowe'en, Johnny. Jessie's been out in the barn winnowing so that she could see her future husband.'

'Ho! and you told me that spitting in the basin was a silly old habit. Well, well. You're to be an old maid. Never mind. You can keep house for me all your days.'

'No, I won't,' she cried. 'I'm not yet fifteen, I'll see him next year.'

'Maybe yes, maybe no. Did the lasses do this when you were young, Stepmither?'

'Most of them,' answered Mrs Brough.

'You too?'

'Me too.'

'You likely saw the young laird.'

'Not him.'

'Well, tell us about it. It's all rubbish anyway.'

She thought for a moment, remembering a Hallowe'en, many years ago it seemed to her now.

'Don't make up a story. You saw nobody,' said Johnny.

She began. 'It's eleven years ago this very night. I was a servant in this house. Your mother was ill, and had been for long. Your father was in Kirkwall with beasts he was selling, and was not coming home that night. I had put you, Jessie, in your cot, and I was waiting for you, Johnny, to go to sleep, while your mother dozed in that chair you're sitting in. I was all set on going out to the barn, and when all three of you were sleeping, I slipped to the dresser, took out the big scissors, and slipped out, making no noise. I ran to the barn, opened both doors, and put the scissors in the sieve. I began to winnow, slowly at first, and then faster, counting the times the sieve went round. Ninety-nine times I whirled it, and hoping to see the young servant lad I had a fancy for, looked out.'

She stopped, living again that moment of expectancy.

'You saw your sweetheart,' said Jessie eagerly.

'You saw no one, just like Jessie.'

'I did not see my young man. Your father passed by the barn door just at that moment, and spoiled things. Back I hurried to the house. Your mother had come out of her doze, and was coughing, as she often did. She looked very frail. Thinking to cheer her up with the arrival of your father when he was not expected home, I said, "Mistress, the master's back. I saw him pass the barn door."

She looked at me sadly for a long time. She knew what I had been doing. At last she said, 'Be good to my bairns." '

She stopped; the young folks expected her to finish the story. Johnny feeling impatient, said, 'Our father would have come in then.'

'No, your father was in Kirkwall.'

'It was not him you saw,' mumbled Jessie.

'It was his living image. Your mother died that winter. My young man took up with another lass, and never came near me. Your father, anxious about you two, urged me to marry him. I wanted to look after you, motherless bairns, and I could not go against your mother's request, or against the shears of fate.'

After a minute Jessie said, 'And so you have.'

'So she has what?' asked Johnnie.

'Been good to us, stupid.'

W.T.C.

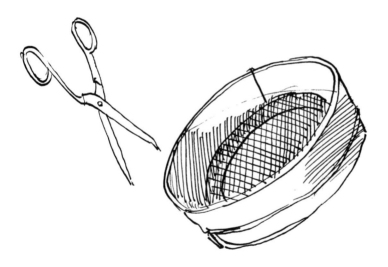

The Black Wife
of Scar

It happened long ago, but old people still spoke of it within living memory. This was the way of it.

Milking time in the byre at Scar, and a dark winter evening. A crusie lamp stood on a stool near Kitto, the milkmaid. Its dim circle of light fell upon her broad back, on her head pressed against the cow's flank. In the dark corners the other beasts stood quietly awaiting their turn to be milked.

The light went out.

'Flecko, thoo beast!' grumbled Kitto crossly. 'Thoo's switched thee tail an' we're all in the dark!'

With that, the light came back.

'Ach, Tam, thee fool!' scolded the girl, sure that the stable lad had crept in to frighten her. 'Stop thee tricks!' But there was no answering guffaw.

'I'll tell the mistress, Tam,' threatened Kitto as the light wavered again. She turned her head sharply against the cow's flank to catch the prankster. The little yellow flame was burning steadily, and no one was in sight.

Then, out of nowhere came a hand, a slim dark hand that cupped itself about the flame, lifting it off the wick, closing about it. . . . The Black Wife of Scar was at her tricks once more.

The Black Wife . . . ? Her story would seem to be part of an episode in the life of a certain Laird of Scar, and may well have gone like this. . . .

Embarking at Calcutta on the first lap of his five-month

voyage home by Indiaman, the Laird of Scar had believed himself well rid of the Black Wife. After twenty-odd very successful years in India, first as a military mercenary and later as a highly-respected East India Company merchant, he was returning to Orkney a wealthy man. His fortune had been made in the ways that such fortunes were made in those years prior to 1800; he was, as he told himself, no worse than other men, and cleverer than most. Not much over forty, he could well afford his modest ambitions for the future. He planned to renovate or rebuild his ancestral home of Scar, installing there a wife, young, Scottish, pretty and well-dowered. True, he had not yet met Mistress Jean, but her father, an East India Company official in high place in Calcutta, favoured the idea of the Laird as son-in-law. With such excellent reason for returning home, he had hastened to set his Indian affairs in order.

Following the profitable sale of his Bengal estates, he paid off and dismissed some sixty-five native servants. That left but four members of his household to arrange for: the dark, nervous boy of sixteen, the little girls of eight and ten, and the mother of all three. The children had caused him no trouble. A brief session with the Company lawyers, a word spoken, an agreement signed, a sum deposited – and the boy, dazed and submissive, was assured of a good future in the Company's service. There followed an interview with the mistress of a well-known and expensive girls' boarding school, a second generous sum on deposit for fees, allowances, and (eventually) dowries – and the little dark-eyed girls were equally well provided for. In both instances, the Laird stressed that all communication was to be made only through the Company's agents and then only in case of death or marriage.

There had remained only their mother to deal with, the former Kashmiri dancing girl. She had been a gift to the Laird (along with a bag of gold coins) from a native prince for whom he had done some favour twenty years before. Her beauty had faded over the years, her temper had worsened, and the Laird was very tired of her. She faced him furiously, her black eyes blazing.

'My children! What have you done with my children?'

'You have told me too often that they were *my* children,' answered the Laird smoothly. 'I have provided for them as *I* think fit.'

'Where . . . ?'

'That does not concern you. *Leave them alone.* If you follow them, they will have nothing from me, and be nothing.'

The Kashmiri considered this in silence, and the Laird explained that her house, her pension, and a conveyance awaited her some miles up the country on the Kashmir road. She ignored him, becoming at once suspiciously submissive.

'I will go with you,' she said quietly, eyes downcast.

'That you will not!' snapped the Laird. 'I go to my own country over the sea. There is no place for you.'

He was a cruel man in anger. The woman departed in silence, and the Laird boarded the Indiaman congratulating himself upon his successful conduct of a potentially embarrassing situation. He welcomed the thought of the five-month voyage around the Cape. A few days' sail, a week off Madras, and the great vessel was under way. Pacing the deck in the evenings, the Laird watched the phosphorescent wake slip behind, awaiting the moment when the blazing tropical stars would set for ever and Arthur's Wain swing up into a pale northern sky. The injured seagull perched in the rigging and fed by passengers and crew reminded him of Orkney beaches and green fields and the fresh sea winds.

Two weeks later he was appalled to find the Kashmiri awaiting him near his cabin. She had come aboard as a lady's *ayah* at Madras.

'Back you go on the next vessel,' he muttered with a curse.

'Alive or dead, I follow you!' said the woman. 'You have left me nothing else.' And she vanished like a bad dream to her duties in the Ladies' Cabin.

The Laird's evening walks became a continuing night-mare. From any secluded corner the veiled and shrouded figure was likely to emerge. Even by daylight he caught her dark malicious glance. That his matrimonial hopes were the subject of shipboard gossip soon became apparent in the increased malignance of her attitude as they exchanged their few bitter words in the cool of the evening.

'*I* am your wife!' she asserted boldly. 'I will tell these white-faced women so if they talk thus!'

'I have no wife,' gritted the Laird.

'*I* am the mother of your children,' she taunted another day.

'No children bear my name,' responded the Laird doggedly. This was quite true: the Laird had prudently supplied them with new names as well as new homes. The Kashmiri flung away angrily as some sailors approached.

'Alive or dead, I follow you!' was her continual refrain, until the dark night that the maddened Laird seized her savagely as she turned away. Pinning her arms to her sides, he pulled the dark veil tight, jerked her head back, carried her to the side. With a final cruel wrench on the fabric, he dropped the light body overboard and saw it break the phosphorescence of the following wave and vanish for ever. Overhead the gull squawked harshly once, twice. Then all was still. The Laird straightened his rumpled coat and went into his cabin.

No alarm was raised, and little attention paid to the disappearance of a very incompetent *ayah*. Within days the whole episode thinned like a dream.

On arrival in London the Laird presented himself, bearing gifts, and was graciously received by Madam Ogilvie. Mistress Jean, fifteen, hazel-eyed and bonny, seemed at first not unwilling. But on the second day of their acquaintance, she burst suddenly and irrationally into tears, sobbing that a cold, invisible hand had grasped hers as she held it out to her betrothed on parting. Worse followed. The next evening, screaming hysterically, she claimed that the hand – a thin brown hand – had appeared from nowhere and extinguished her bedside candle. Seriously perturbed, her mother arrested the preparations for the wedding, returned the pearls and the diamond bracelets to the Laird for better safekeeping, and took her daughter to Bath for a rest cure.

Gloomily the Laird acquiesced in her decision. Gloomily he travelled north to Scar, not perhaps, unaccompanied. Two months later he quietly accepted the breaking of the marriage agreement (after which Mistress Jean recovered completely).

The Laird renovated his House of Scar, but did not long remain in it. He had trouble keeping servants; he did not marry. He fared somewhat better in the new mansion, it is said, but realized few of his ambitions. Of his later years but one tradition survives: he hated the cry of the gulls and spent long hours on the beach shooting them. It was his only diversion.

And the Black Wife? She made her presence known at intervals in the byre – the slim dark hand coming out of nowhere, cupping itself about the flame, lifting it off the wick, closing about it. . . . And putting it back.

M.N.C.

Gramarye, Fog, and Fire

When her mother called her to get up and light the fire, Daisy o' the Meadows rose on a Sunday morning in no pious mood. She had not slept well. Her father was in the byre feeding the cattle. When the fire was going, her mother rose, and together they made breakfast and set the table. Her father, Hugh Swanney, came in and sat down.

'Young Harcus must have spent the night with Meg o' Hoosay,' he said. 'He was legging it home to Grindally when I went out. Meg must have done you out o' your big bold young man, Daisy. Didn't I hear him speak to you at the door late last night?'

'Yes, Father, and I sent him away. I told him he could go to Hoosay.'

'Deed, and I think you did,' broke in Mrs Swanney. 'A loose lad, that Jock Harcus. No like Davie o' Hool.'

Daisy tossed her head, saying, 'I don't want either of them.'

'Weel, we'll see,' said her father. 'Noo we must get ready for the kirk.'

As they walked to the kirk, they were joined by Davie Shearer, just as they passed the croft of Hoosay. Daisy and her mother walked in front, the two men following and talking about the weather and the ploughing. They drew near to the low, thatch-roofed cottage of Gruttill, and, from the low door, a little old woman dressed in black stared at them out of black eyes in a thin wrinkled face.

'Good morning, Babbo, and how are you keeping?' called out Mrs Swanney cheerily.

No answer came; only a steady malevolent stare out of those black eyes.

'What's wrong with her, Hugh?' asked his wife when they had passed on. 'She seems to be putting a spell on us.'

'Oh,' laughed Hugh, 'I had words with her last week when I was mending the roof on Backaskaill. When I was up on the ladder, I asked her why she didn't come to the kirk on Sundays like a decent body. She glared knives at me and screamed, "I'm praying to the devil, Hugh Swanney, that you fall off that ladder and break your neck." "Dunno do that, woman," I said, "for I have a sma' job to do for thee yet." "For me? And what's that?" "Dig a hole to put thee in." ' Hugh laughed as he finished.

'Hugh, you should not have said that,' admonished Mrs Swanney. 'She's a real witch.'

'Witch, and you a Christian woman, wife, believing in such frootery!'

'A Christian woman I am, and I believe that the Bad One has his servants here, and she's one of them.'

'Ach!'

As they walked on, a gig sounded behind them. Harcus of Grindally drove past, and with him were Meg Matches o' Hoosay and her parents. Daisy kept her eyes on the ground as the pony sped past, leaving the others to return the greetings from the gig. When they entered the kirk, Daisy passed the pew in which the Matches were seated, her eyes fixed on the floor. Her mother and she sat in a pew in which there were two others. Her father and Davie sat in front of them. At the last moment, just as the Reverend Mathew entered, Jock Harcus squeezed in beside Daisy. All through the prayers, the readings, and the sermon, she felt the pressure of his shoulder against her. In the hymn singing, he looked on with her, for he had no hymnary. Furious as Daisy felt, she had to admire his fine singing voice. But she longed for the doxology and blessing, so that she could get away from his disturbing pressure. He had chosen Meg. If he thought she was taking Meg's leavings, he was mistaken.

At last they were dismissed, Daisy not feeling she was blessed, and, as she left, Harcus politely stepped aside to let her and her mother pass. At the door she grasped her mother's arm, and almost dragged her to the road where she started walking fast. Not until they heard her father and Davie behind them did she let go.

'Lass,' said Mrs Swanney, 'you gripped me that hard one would think the devil was after me.'

'Or after me,' murmured Daisy.

'Surely not coming out o' the kirk,' laughed Davie.

'Well, folks say he keeks in the kirk door to see if he can catch them that's no paying attention,' added Hugh.

A gig whirled past them, no greeting coming from it. Harcus was saying something in Meg's ear, and she was laughing. Daisy slowed her pace, her mother chatting away, and she answering in monosyllables. At the cottage of Gruttill, there was old Babbo, staring at them with seeming malevolence. Daisy glanced at her mother's face; it was serious and a little worried. Mrs Swanney turned to her husband and said, 'Hugh, I wish you had not said that to Babbo. I'm sure she's trying to put a curse on you.'

'Never a hair I care for her curses. Frootery! What the minister calls ignorant superstition!'

As they went on, Mrs Swanney whispered to Daisy, 'I hope we are not made to suffer.'

'Do you think she can cast a spell on us, Mother?'

'Deed and I do. She had a spite against a boatman, and she upset the boat in the Ronaldsay Firth, and three men were drowned.'

'Upset the boat! How could she do that?'

'She floated a wooden scoop in the churn, and said a spell. The milk whirled around, and the scoop filled and sank. At the same minute, the boat filled and sank off the Riv, and the sea was calm. It happened before you were born, lass.'

'Three men were actually drowned on a fine day?'

'Yes. That old wife does the deil's own work for him.'

Daisy thought for a time and then asked, 'How could she harm Father?'

'In lots o' ways. She can put a blight on our crops, and make our beasts sicken, and your father as well.'

'Father! In what way?'

'Oh, she'll make a sma' likeness of him in clay or candle wax, and stick pins in it, and say her spell that will give him the fits.'

'Lord preserve us,' breathed Daisy, and walked on in silence. At Hoosay, she noted that a gig and pony were tied up; Harcus was having dinner with the Matches. At the Meadows, Mrs Swanney invited Davie Shearer to stay for dinner. He thanked her, but said his old folks would miss him, and his mother laid great store by the Sunday dinner.

'Do we no all,' answered Mrs Swanney, and Davie passed on.

Daisy did not put great store by the Sunday dinner that followed. Her mind was in a turmoil. She had never expected that Jock Harcus would go to Meg o' Hoosay last night. Now he was with her. Her mother was right in thinking him a loose character. But oh! that fine singing voice, that tall upright figure, and those bold, manly features.

As the evening wore on, she worried more and more about the harm Babbo Gruttill could do to her father. At night she dreamed. Her father was sitting helpless in his chair, groaning. She woke up to hear him snore peacefully at the other side of the partition. Again she fell asleep, and again she dreamed the same dream just before she awoke to hear her father call her in his usual cheery way to rise and light the fire. Her mother rose, and after a little said, 'You're looking right poorly this morning, lass. What's the matter?'

'Nothing really, Mother, but I dreamed twice last night that Babbo Gruttill had put a spell on Father, and he was groaning in pain.'

'He's well and hearty. She's no started her tricks yet, anyway; but she will, and only the Lord can stop her.'

Listlessly Daisy set the table while her mother prepared breakfast. Hugh Swanney came in and looked closely at her. 'You're looking as if the trows had got you, Daisy.'

'The little folks? No, I did not sleep very well, that's all.'

'Ha, jealous of Meg o' Hoosay taking Harcus away from you.'

'She can have him,' snapped Daisy.

'Don't get mad about it, then. Wife, is the breakfast no ready yet?'

'This very minute, Hugh. Are your beasts fine this morning?'

'Of course. I look after them well.'

'Aye, you do that. But beasts go wrong in times.'

'Ours are not going wrong,' Hugh said brusquely, annoyed at the implication that he could not look after his animals. He sat down and began eating his porridge with gusto.

'You've no salted this enough,' he said angrily, and his hand shot out for the salt dish, and sent it flying.

'That's bad luck,' cried Mrs Swanney. 'Throw some over your left shoulder.'

'I'll watch it. More frootery,' growled her husband.

The little incident, however seemed to have annoyed him, for he was silent, and went out to the plough, banging the door. When the dishes were washed, and the house tidied, Mrs Swanney said she was going over to Hool, to see how old Mrs Shearer was keeping.

Daisy's unease grew when she was left alone in the house. Occasionally she felt anger over Harcus, but chiefly she brooded over possible harm Babbo Gruttill could do her father. This fear played so strongly on her that she determined to go and plead with the old witch. Taking her little money, three half-crowns, a shilling, and a threepenny piece with her in order to buy the witch's favour, she set off, resolutely looking straight in front of her as she passed Hoosay. Men were ploughing in a large field of Warsetter, and one man was ploughing in a field of Boloquoy, near Grunavi Head, the only high part in sight of the western shore of the island. At the Knowes, a man was ploughing with a horse and an ox. Having passed the croft of Cliff, she came soon to Gruttill.

The low door was ajar. Daisy glanced in. Babbo, seated on a stool, was bent over the open fire which sent up long, thin, blue flames. In her hands was a lump of candle wax that dripped its meltings into the fire. The witch was modelling this into the shape of a person. She finished making it, held it out to cool, and cackled in laughter. The model was about four inches high. Now, Babbo took pins from a pincushion lying near, and stuck some into the figure, saying, 'Into your skin, Hugh Swanney.' She pushed them a little farther in. 'Into your flesh, Hugh Swanney.' Again. 'Into your sinew, Hugh Swanney, and now. . . .' Daisy banged the door fully open. 'Babbo, Babbo,' she cried, 'don't say it.'

The witch straightened and turned, looking unblinkingly at the girl with black, evil eyes below black eye-brows and coal-black hair.

'And why no,' Babbo said in a flat voice. Then she screeched, 'The man that's waiting aroond to dig a pit to put me in!'

'Ah, Babbo, he did not mean it. I'll give you money . . .'

'He said it, and has aye laughed at me saying I have no power to work weal or ill. I'll . . .' The black eyes glinted. 'Money? How much?'

Daisy poured the contents of her purse into her own palm. 'That's all I've got.'

Babbo glanced contemptuously at the three half-crowns, the shilling, and the threepenny. 'It'll take more than that,' she said through her toothless gums.

'But I've got no more.'

'Your mither will have it in a jar. Take it all and come back.'

'Steal from my mother. I'll no do it for all the evil you can work.'

'Wait till your milk turns blue, your beasts sicken, and that fither o' your shakes with the ague.'

'I'm no stealing, and besides Father keeps the purse.'

Babbo Gruttill stared with her black eyes, and said nothing for a while. Despair lay at Daisy's heart. Finally Babbo reached out her skinny hand and said, 'Give me all of it.'

'You'll not work harm on us,' said Daisy eagerly.

'Give me all and I'll tell you.' Babbo stretched out her hand.

Daisy emptied all the money into the claw-armed, wizened hand. The old woman looked at it, and then took the threepenny piece and held it out to Daisy, saying, 'Take this back, and I'll tell you.'

The girl took the coin.

'Now you must buy a book from me that will give you great power, especially over your rival, Meg o' Hoosay, and over Jock Harcus. You will give me the coin for the book.'

'Shall my father be safe?' asked Daisy impatiently.

'Safe as long as you keep the book and use the power you will get by obeying its orders. You will keep it until you sell it to one for a white coin less than this.'

'But there are no white coins less than a threepenny.'

'There are, and very old ones. Someone will have them. Take my offer or suffer what will come.' Babbo brought out a small, square, black book from a drawer under the small window.

Daisy looked at the book with misgivings.

'Your father will be safe, or . . .'

'Here's the coin. Give me the book,' cried Daisy in desperation.

She handed over the coin, slipped the book under her coat, and hurried out. Behind her sounded an evil cackle, 'He! He! He!'

Daisy ran from the cottage, but soon had to walk. Having got her breath back, she wondered what could be in this ominous book. The bad, she felt sure; but, if so, she need not read it. As she drew nearer home, the book seemed to grow heavy, and she wondered if she could carry it much farther. At last she was inside. Her mother had not returned. Daisy hurried to her room, and drew the book from under her jacket. It was quite light; she must have imagined it being heavy. As she put it under her pillow, she looked at it with horror.

The outer door opened. She left her room, but did not tell her mother that she had been out. Hurriedly she asked how Mrs Shearer was, and her mother replied that the old woman was poorly but not seriously ill.

'What a good son Davie is to his ailing mother and father!' exclaimed Mrs Swanney. Daisy knew this was a hint, but neither Davie nor Harcus was in her mind. That black book! What could be in it. She endured a fearful anxiety throughout the day. At last it came bed time, and she went to her room, and lit the paraffin lamp.

The black book had black pages with white print. The first page told her that the devil would give her great power if she gave herself completely to him. Then followed instructions. At the dead of night she must go to the shore and lie down below the tide mark. She must stretch out her hands and her feet, put stones on them and on her chest, and say

Mester Fiend, I lay me doon.
Take me body, take me a'
Fae the soles o' me feet to the tap o' me croon
Take me, thou great Wallawa.

Daisy shuddered. She turned over a page which told her how to make a love potion to capture a sweetheart. One line of disgusting matter was all she could stand. How was she to get rid of the evil thing? No one she knew would have an old coin less in value than a threepenny. Besides, she did not want anyone, good or bad, to have this vile thing. She turned over another page of the fearful book to see circles, triangles, and printing below these. She closed it and thrust it under her pillow. Tomorrow she would burn it before her mother rose.

She slept only for minutes at a time; between, in her waking moments, fear clutched at her. Would that evil

woman leave her father sane and healthy? Her cackle had
sounded ominous. No trust could be put in her promise. If
only morning would come and she could see the foul thing
devoured in the flames. She dozed off, exhausted by her
fears.

'Daisy! This is the second time I've called you. Rise,
lass, and light the fire.'

'Yes, Father,' called Daisy as she jumped from her bed.
At once she set the kindling alight, and put on two coals,
her hands and body shaking. She hurried to her bed, and
carried the book to the stove, and held it over the flames.
It did not kindle; it did not smoulder no matter how she
thrust it into the fire. She heard her mother get up.
Hurriedly she put the book back under her pillow, and
finished stoking the fire. During breakfast, her parents
chatted amiably, not noticing how distraught their
daughter was. Again Mrs Swanney sang Davie Shearer's
praises, telling how attentive he was to his folks. Hugh
Swanney said he ought to give Davie help with the
ploughing as the year was getting on. Breakfast was at last
over. Hugh Swanney went out to his ploughing, and her
mother and Daisy tidied up. Mrs Swanney took up her
knitting. Daisy said she would go down to the shore to see
if there was any driftwood on the beach. Putting the black
book under her coat, she went down the road until she was
opposite Grunavi Head. As she turned to cross the field,
she thought for a moment that a short, black figure
appeared in the distance, but either it disappeared or she
had imagined she saw it. Down at the high headland, she
stood for a minute at the cliff edge, watching huge billows
roll in foam over the rocks, and then she flung the black
book seaward with all her strength. It fluttered in the air,
its leaves spread out, and then it fell gradually, like a
preying black skua, into the waves, and disappeared.

Daisy turned homeward with a light step. Suddenly she
stopped. Was that the short black figure again? No,
nothing was there. She went home, a weight lifted from her
soul. Her mother was still knitting. Daisy went to her

room, and turned down the pillow to have the pleasure of seeing nothing under it.

There lay the black book.

Black despair clutched at the heart of the girl. Down she sank on a stool, stifling a scream, and gasped for breath. On recovering a little, one thought filled her mind; she must not burden her parents with her grief. Mechanically she set the table for the mid-day meal. Her father came in to announce, 'I'm ploughing for Davie this afternoon. His folks are feeling better, but they're tired of Davie's cooking. Wife, go over at four, and make dinner for them. I'll unyoke later, and have dinner with you. Daisy, you make a good dinner for Davie, and we'll send him over – that is, if you don't want to entertain Jock Harcus.'

'No, Father, I'm never going to entertain Jock. Tell Davie I am expecting him.'

Davie! she thought. Yes, he is dependable. I must unburden myself to someone, and he will share my trouble, I know. So she decided.

Her mother left about four. At six, in the darkening, Davie came, and she welcomed him with a wan smile, the chill at her heart receding. Davie, as usual, was shy, and though he saw something was bothering Daisy, he tried to converse about ordinary matters, weather, farm work, and neighbours. With supper finished and the table cleared, she sat down and told the young man all her troubles. Davie did not say a word throughout, or utter an exclamation. When he sat with his head down after she had finished, she wondered if he simply felt repelled by her actions, or did he think she had made her bed and must lie on it. At last he looked up and at her, saying solemnly, 'Daisy, I wish I could do something for you, but this is bad beyond my mending.' He stopped. Was that all he could say?

Davie cleared his throat. 'The only help I can think of is with the minister. Take that cursed book and we'll go to see Mr Mathew. If you don't want to tell him, I'll do it for you.'

'The minister! What can he do, Davie.'

'He'll know what to do. He will say a prayer that will stop the badness. Let's go.'

A faint hope crept into Daisy's soul. Taking her coat and putting the black book inside it, she and Davie set off in the dark, north on the road to the manse. After a mile, Daisy spoke. 'I'm feared to go near Gruttill, Davie. We'll go down to the east crags until we get well past it, and then back to the road.'

'All right, Daisy. We turn east here and face the hill. Then we go down to the shore.'

At the crest of the hill they saw a wall of fog rolling seaward.

'Strange,' muttered Davie. 'It should be going the other way.'

'It will hide us from Babbo, Davie. My, it's so thick we can't see a thing.'

'We'll turn north to the fence that runs down, and follow the fence on the shore, until we come to the sand, and then angle up across the links.'

They did so, going into a mist as thick as soup. As they followed the shore line fence, they ran into fog as thick and as black as molasses, and this was just below Gruttill. 'Davie, we'll lose our way and fall over the cliffs,' wailed Daisy, as she stopped.

'Never fear, Daisy lass. I could find this path with my eyes shut. But do you feel the awful smell?'

'Yes, I never felt one so bad. Did you see that?'

'What?'

'A spark went overhead. There's more. They look like little red devils.'

For a minute or two they watched. The stench grew worse. Daisy clung to Davie.

'Come, lass, we'll get out of here,' he said hoarsely, and pulled her along. Then he led her down a path to the sand, and along to the links. As they angled across to the road, the fog cleared, the stench had gone, and the seven stars of the Plough came out along with others. The two breathed more freely, but hurried on. At last they came to the manse, in which they were glad to see lighted windows. Mr Mathew had not retired.

He answered their knock. 'Oh, Mr Mathew, I'm in sore trouble. Only you can help me.'

The tall, broad-shouldered clergyman looked at the couple with distaste. The usual trouble of young un-married couples, he thought, and them of respectable families. Aloud he said grumpily, 'Come into my study, and tell me your trouble.'

Chilled by this reception, the two followed him to his study and seated themselves. Daisy tried to begin, but stammered, and was silent.

'Tell me, David,' the minister said brusquely.

Davie told briefly how and why Daisy had the black book, how she had tried to get rid of it and failed, and that she had read little and used none of the contents. At his advice they had come to their pastor.

'The Almighty defend us!' breathed the minister. 'To think such evil exists in my God-fearing parish.' Then, firmly. 'Give me that book.'

Daisy, a load removed from her soul, handed it over at once. Mr Mathew held it, and looked at it with loathing. 'You said this book would not burn. We shall see. Davie, go and start a fire on the road. Use straw and some wood you'll find outside.'

Davie went at once. As soon as the minister saw it blazing, he signed to Daisy to come, and holding the book at arm's length they went to the fire. Mr Mathew held the book above the flames, and murmured, 'My God, this is no holy bush of Moses but the work of the Enemy. Oh, Lord, let it be consumed.' He flung the black book into the fire.

For a time it spluttered and repelled the flames, and a foul smell came from it. This caused Davie to look towards the road they had come, for it was the same stench he had felt below Gruttill. He thought he saw a reflection over Fea Hill, and blue beams shoot up, which flickered and fell. He turned to the others. The black book was burning, and dissolving into grey ashes. When it was wholly consumed,

Mr Mathew said to Daisy, 'You were to be the victim sacrificed on the altar of the Enemy. But you did not yield to the evil, and, now the book is destroyed, the evil will recoil on the head of the mover.'

'Oh, Mr Mathew, you have saved me!' exclaimed Daisy.

'Not me, your Maker has, and may His Grace, Mercy, and Peace go with you both. Goodnight.'

As they walked swiftly homeward, Davie had forgotten about the blue rays he had seen over Fea Hill. As they neared Babbo's abode, they saw only a glow, like that which came from a huge kelp pit that had burned all the seaweed and tangles. They caught their breaths. Gruttill lay in glowing embers, and a group of neighbours were gathered around. Rob o' the Cliff shouted to them before they were opposite the ruins.

'Gruttill's gone, and Babbo wi' it. Both burned to cinders.'

After a minute Davie asked, thinking of what the minister said about the evil recoiling, 'Did she set fire to her own house?'

'Best kens,' said Rob. 'No doubt she was making images of some one she had a spite against. Of candle wax. She was aye at it, trying to plague first one and then another.'

After standing stupified for some time, the two moved on.

'Terrible,' murmured Daisy. 'Poor old body.'

'The minister said the evil would recoil on the head of the mover,' Davie said sombrely. 'She was a wicked woman. Now your father will have to dig a pit for her bones, as he said he would.'

W.T.C.

The Stolen Winding-Sheet

Old Baubie Skithawa lay dying. She had long been feeble, but she had enough to keep her, and waṡ beholden to no one. Baubie had prepared well for her burying. Her grave clothes were laid by in her chest; long since she had bought a fine winding-sheet at the Lammas Fair.

Knowing that her days were short, old Baubie called for Jenny, the midwife, who not only brought people into the world but also helped with laying out the corpses. So Baubie called for Jennie now, and says she,

'Lass, I'm wanting to show you where to lay your hand on my grave clothes when the time comes. And I'd like to be sure that I have all that is needed. I don't want to go ill-clad to my grave, for I've always tried to do things decently. Do you think I should try them on?'

'No, no!' says Jennie, 'I can tell fine by the look of them whether they'll do or no.'

When she saw them, she thought they would do very well. She said that she had dressed many a corpse in Sanday, but never had she seen better grave clothes on any. Baubie died soon afterwards, and Jenny laid her out in all her fine grave clothes. The neighbours sat two nights at the lykewake, and among them was the goodwife of Bae. A rough, coarse sort she was; everyone called her Black Jock after her old grandfather who was said to be close kin to the Devil himself. Folks noticed that Black Jock often fingered the winding-sheet, and once she muttered,

'It's a great pity to put such a fine piece of cloth under the mold.'

But no one replied. Black Jock had no friends and people were afraid to cross her. She too was thought to be over-friendly with Old Nick. Black Jock was there when Baubie was put into the coffin, and she drank her fill at the wake afterwards.

Now what did Black Jock do a day or two afterwards? Down to the Cross Kirk graveyard she went in the silence of the night, with a spade in her hand. She dug up Baubie Skithawa's grave; she broke open the coffin lid; and she took the fine winding-sheet off the poor dead body. Then she filled up the grave, and home she went and laid the stolen winding-sheet away at the bottom of her own chest.

The very next day the Lady of Hellsness sent Andrew Moodie on an errand to Stove. As he was coming back in the mirky dusk, the sky grew black as the bottom of a kettle, and when Andrew was half over Bae Sand there broke out the most fearful storm of thunder and lightning that ever he saw. Fire leaped from cloud to cloud, flashing to sea and ground like sparks from the forge. The thunder crashed as if the very heavens were rumbling down for Judgment Day. Andrew noticed that the cloud was blacker over the Cross Kirk than anywhere else, and when he came near, for his road ran beside the kirkyard, he saw a sight that almost made him faint with terror.

From every grave in the kirkyard, there stood up something like a mast of fire, red, yellow, blue. And the tops of these pillars of fire were far above the kirk roof. Sometimes the pillars of coloured flame stood straight on end; sometimes they waved from side to side like reeds in a breeze. On the top of every pillar stood one or two, and sometimes three or four, spirits of the dead, fluttering in their grave clothes. And the spirits beckoned and waved to one another, or shook their heads at each other as if they had been a flock of ducks. If they were speaking, Andrew did not know, for he heard not a word. But on top of one of the

fiery pillars he saw one poor forlorn spirit standing motion-
less and alone – and she was bare naked. That was Baubie
Skithawa's spirit, whose winding-sheet was stolen. And all
the rest were glowering and pointing at poor Baubie as if
they were scolding or making fun of her. For it is said
that if spirits come back to the world (may they stay in
their own place!) they just take up their old ways and
habits.

Andrew feared that Baubie's spirit was about to look at
him, and he turned his back to the kirk. Well he knew that
a ghost's glance is not canny and has stolen the sense of
many. No farther would he go – not for all the gold in the
king's chest would he go by that kirkyard. So he made for
the house of Bae as fast as his trembling legs would move,
and banged and kicked on the door with all the strength
left to him. And he cried.

'For heaven's sake open the door. I've seen things tonight that I'll never be the better of! And if ever you hope
for mercy, have pity on me! Open the door! No, I never
saw the like in all my life . . .!'

Black Jock was in her house alone, for her goodman had
gone to visit a sick cousin at Rusness. He was a poor stick,
the goodman of Bae; Black Jock had fairly scared what
little sense he had out of him. But still, he had enough to
bide at Rusness that wild night.

Whatever Black Jock was thinking, she took Andrew in.
Then she banged the door shut again and barred it with the
wooden yoke she used for carrying water pails. Andrew
noticed that three steel awls were sticking in the wood. And
she said to him.

'What the Devil takes you out on such a night? Idle
whelp that you are! Sit over there on the stool, and mind –
a close tongue keeps a safe head!'

The moment that she said the Evil One's name there
came a clap of thunder right over the roof and such a blaze
of lightning that Andrew was both stunned and blinded.
When he recovered a little, he saw Black Jock sitting in the
middle of the floor, drawing circles around her with a big

needle. Her lips were moving and her face was dark and troubled. Andrew was about to tell her what he had seen at the kirk, but the minute he opened his mouth, she picked up a hard peat and clouted him. It caught him on the knee and he shrieked with pain. But short time he had to think of that!

For now, between the crashes of thunder, he heard outside the house of Bae, a noise like the jabber of a thousand scolding folk, but they spoke no earthly tongue. The smoke-hole, the window, and the cat-hole through the eaves at the top of the door had all three been stopped by Black Jock's own hands. Now every bit of stopping was being driven out by ghostly hands. And again and again he saw the ghostly face of Baubie Skithawa's spirit glowering through the window-hole. And O, that face was white, white! And always the spirit cried with a doleful whimper,

'Cold, cold, am I the night! Cold, cold am I! Give me my sheet! Give me my sheet! It's cold, cold, to lie in the mold, mother-naked! Give me my sheet!'

And then she shrieked fit to rend the heart of any living creature. The cat lay trembling and howling in a corner, for the dumb beasts cannot abide ghosts. Then one of the spirits thrust in his hand through the cat-hole and pulled out the old shearing-hook that Black Jock had put over the door to keep away evil spirits. He pulled it out, but he let it drop at once, for there was steel in the hook. Then he set up such a roar that Andrew thought the very ghosts themselves had gone mad. And they began again, dancing like devils about the house, around the house, over the house and under and on the house, roaring like mad bulls. It was getting near cock-crow, and well they knew their time was short.

Once Baubie's spirit thrust her head and long neck through the window, and then she got in her two long white arms and kept groping through and groping through the house, and peering about in search. One of her arms came feeling about over Andrew's head, and he cowered down in mortal fear. For all that, he got one wallop from

her hand on the crown of his head, and the mark stood
there all his life. When he felt the ghostly blow, he fell on
the floor, and the toe of his shoe flicked the sail-needle out
of Black Jock's hand. Then she swore a fearful oath, for she
knew well that the spirits would have their way now that
she lacked the steel. She had no time to delay: she flung
open her big chest and dragged the winding-sheet out from
the bottom. No sooner was the sheet free of the chest than
it flipped out of her hands like a living thing. And up it flew,
and around and around it whirled, and out of the smoke-
hole in a blaze of blue fire.

'The Devil himself go with thee and bide with thee!'
cursed Black Jock as the sheet switched out of the hole. No
sooner was the word out of her mouth when *something* gave
her a great wallop on the rear, flinging her flat on her face
on the earth floor.

At that blessed moment the cock crew, and the spirits
flew off to their own place. Andrew heard them fluttering
overhead like a flock of frightened swans.

When the folk came to the house of Bae in the dawn,
they found the place in dreadful disorder. Everything was
flung here and yon, and the three cattle lay dead in the
byre. Andrew Moodie was lying helpless as if half-dead,
with the mark of Baubie Skithawa's spirit's thumb and
finger on the crown of his head. He recovered well enough,
but never a hair grew on that mark afterwards.

The folk tried to lift Black Jock from the ground where
the spirits had flung her. They lifted and they pulled, they
tugged and they heaved, but they could not budge her,
although five women and three men tried with all their
strength. You see, she was spirit-bound, or as some say,
she had the ghost-cramp. They did not like to send for the
minister, for they did not know how he would take it. So off
they bustled for old Mansie Peace, the grandfather of Peter
Peace who would neither burn nor drown. All those folk
had more wit than their own.

Old Mansie went around Black Jock seven times, and
said seven eerisons over her. Then he boiled seven blue

stones and made enchanted water of the brew, and poured a full measure of it over Black Jock's back. And then she could rise, for the water took the ghost-cramp off her.

W.T.C.

The Hogboon of Hell

About the middle of last century a certain Patrick McVicar was presented by the laird to the Presbytery of the Church of Scotland in Orkney, approved, and inducted as the minister of St Colms in succession to Mr Hutchison who had died. The parishioners had loved their old minister, who was kindly and eloquent, and were therefore ready to look upon his successor with a critical eye.

At first they had trouble in understanding Mr McVicar. His native language was Gaelic so that his accent and his arrangement of sentences were strange to them. 'When the postman will he be passing?' had to be understood as 'When will the postman be passing?' For his first sermon he gave forth the text: Be sober, be vigilant; because your adversary the devil, as a roaring lion, walketh about, seeking whom he may devour. Having read it over twice, first in low tones, and then almost shouting it, he began; 'Brethren, first we must ask who, the Devil, he was; secondly, where, the Devil, he was going; and thirdly what, the Devil, he was roaring about?' Red-faced parents hushed their tittering children in the pews. The minister's fluency in English, however, increased rapidly with his having to talk it every day, and also, unfortunately, the length of his sermons. His flock resigned themselves to long sermons; it was another matter that troubled them.

As part of his stipend, Mr McVicar had the benefit of a glebe, a fair-sized tract of land, much of it fertile, other parts not. This glebe was divided into crofts, and the

tenants paid their rents either in cash or in kind. The old minister had been very considerate of his tenants, especially when the crops were poor, or when misfortune struck a family. Mr McVicar, coming in a year when the crops were poor, exacted the last penny, the last pound of meal, and the last half-ounce of butter from them. More, he would not accept the tenants' word for weighing or measuring; that had to be done again on his scales. Several tenants quarrelled with him, but none seriously except Robbie Cursitter, tenant of the large croft of Helye, which had mixed soil in the western part, stony and hilly in the middle, and fertile in the east.

Helye had been a farm away back when Orkney was ruled by Norse earls. Helye-githa, meaning Holy Enclosure, it had been at one time, and it was said that the ruins of a church had once stood near Robbie's house; but, if so, no trace of it remained. The name had been contracted to Helye, and no one bothered about what it meant.

Relations between Cursitter and the minister grew worse, and as a result, at the end of three years, McVicar split the large croft in two, and gave the eastern part to his plough-man, Henry Hay, a docile man, who agreed that his rent should be the working of the minister's home fifteen acres, and the supplying of the McVicar household at the manse with cheese, butter, and meal. When Cursitter was told of this by the minister, he protested vigorously, pointing out that his grown-up son whose services he needed could not live with his parents on half the original Helye, and that Henry Hay, given both the half and the benefit of the minister's home croft, was so favoured that Cursitter would see the laird about it. Mr McVicar agreed reluctantly to split the original in three, Robbie to have the west, his son, Jim, the middle, and Henry Hay the east and fertile portion.

'But the name, Mr McVicar,' said Robbie. 'It is no longer the farm of Helye.'

'Call it that which you like. To me that is of no interest,' snapped the minister.

Henry Hay, now having good prospects, persuaded a girl whom he had long hankered for, to marry him, and began to build a little cottage on his croft, saying that its name was Paradise. Robbie Cursitter continued to call his Helye, and his son Jim said he would wait until he had buildings erected before naming his. Many thought that Hay was rash in naming his croft Paradise until he found it to his liking.

Another misfortune befell Robbie Cursitter shortly after the division. Near the house and steading of Helye there was a mound, and in this mound very old people declared that a mound-dweller called a hogboon lay asleep, and some day would waken. A hogboon is known in other parts as a boggart – a goblin or bugbear. According to the elders, hogboons could be either troublesome and vindictive or friendly and helpful, and all of them were sportive. They could go into hibernation in the mound for weeks, or years, or even centuries. There was no telling when they would wake up. Both Robbie and his wife knew the old legend, but, as they had never been troubled at Helye, they never gave the matter a thought until the hogboon woke up and began to pester them.

While old Mrs Cursitter stood over her churn one day, rhythmically raising and lowering the dasher, the handle began to vibrate violently in her hands. Then the lid flew up, followed by the dasher, and cream scattered all over her clean flag-stoned floor, and into the embers on the hearth, spitting, and smelling as it evaporated. Next the door flew open, and something flashed past her. She thought she caught sight for a moment of a little figure, a man with a beard, wizened, and not more than two feet high; but she was not sure if she actually saw it or imagined it.

Robbie Cursitter was winnowing grain in the barn. He had half-filled the riddle, as he called his coarse sieve, and, while lifting it off the floor, it whirled around in his hands, flew up into the air, and spilt its contents over Robbie. As soon as he recovered from his surprise, he remembered old

tales of hogboons, and called out, 'Here Trim, here Trim.'
A big shaggy dog bounded up. 'Seek him Trim. Trim him,
Trim,' shouted Robbie, but was chagrined to see his dog
leap around and speed away, yelping in pain. It dashed
straight to the water-filled quarry, plunged in under the
water, came up and remained near the edge.

Meanwhile Mrs Cursitter, the better of her fright, had
arranged two nests for her broody hens. She went to a box
under which she had imprisoned the hens, lifted the edge,

and reached in carefully to get a hold on one. A low, husky quack sounded, and she drew out a drake. 'My gracious!' she exclaimed, and flung it from her. Again she reached in and drew out another drake. 'Bless my soul!' she muttered and went to see if the broody hens were on the nests. They were not, and the eggs she had put in were gone.

For three more days the Cursitters were pestered. Milking pails leaked, cream turned sour overnight, pigs squealed, and calves ran galloping around the small pasture as if they had heard the Prodigal Son had returned. On the evening of the third day of torment, when things had been quiet for hours, Jim Cursitter came home after labouring on his croft for days. He now had the walls of a small cottage up, and he would thatch it in autumn. He wanted to start a byre, but had not yet got the stones. Too tired to take much interest, he listened to his parents' tale of woe.

'I chose to keep the name Helye,' shouted Robbie, 'but now it shall be Hell, for that's what it is.'

His son stirred himself. 'That's what I thought of calling my stony bit of ground. But I'll do with Purgatory. Mind you, the minister won't like it.'

'Him!' exclaimed his mother. 'He'll tell folks that he rules Paradise, Purgatory, and Hell.'

Just as she had finished saying this, a window cracked, and broken glass scattered on the floor.

'There goes the hogboon again,' sighed Mrs Cursitter.

'Why don't you put a curse on him, Father?' asked Jim.

'That I will.' Taking a deep breath he shouted: 'Hogboon. Blast your miserable skin. Get out of this place. Go to the devil, your master, or to the minister, for he has a fine mound near his big house on the bay.'

The door opened gently. A low sighing noise lasted for a minute, and the door gently closed.

'He's gone,' exclaimed Robbie, gleefully.

'Aye,' said his wife, 'but the poor thing sighed pitifully at the door.'

'Poor thing! Do you want your windows broken and your cream spilt, and your eggs taken?'

'No, Robbie, but the devil or the minister! That's a sore choice.'

'May be. May be. But Hell is the name I gave this house, and Hell is to be its name.'

'And mine,' added Jim, 'stays Purgatory, aye, even if I ever get all the stones dug up, and break the heather.'

Although Helye had peace when the name was changed to Hell, the old Cursitters had a hard struggle to make ends meet on their small croft, and Robbie grew feeble, allowing the buildings to deteriorate. Jim had little time to spare, for his Purgatory took all of it.

Meanwhile, the hogboon had taken up his abode in the mound on the bay near the fine manse of the Reverend Patrick McVicar. For weeks he lay quiet, making his cell in the mound to his liking. McVicar, ignorant of the mound-dweller, learned with glee that the name of Helye was now Hell, and the other croft Purgatory. As Mrs Cursitter had foretold, he was proud of being the proprietor of Paradise, Purgatory and Hell, and pleased with his home acres worked by Henry Hay. His girth, extensive as it had been, extended more with hearty eating – a large, flabby man with a dog-fish eye, and a loud hectoring voice.

His complacency did not last long. Things began happening at the manse. The butter brought by Mrs Hay, though weighed, tasted, and smelled by the minister, turned rancid overnight; the cheese dissolved into watery curds. The meal which he had weighed and examined turned mouldy. He blustered at poor Henry Hay who stammered that the minister well knew that the produce he and his wife had brought was fresh, clean, and of full weight.

Before long, however, Mr McVicar had to admit that trouble was being caused by something strange and mysterious. On Saturday night he could find only thirty pages of the English translation of his sermon for Sunday, although the forty-five pages of the Gaelic version had not been touched. Sunday came, and the congregation was dismissed with his blessing after being only forty minutes in the pews.

When he arrived back at the manse, after the service he stood outside, examining the windows of his study, and then he examined every window in the manse. There was not a sign of an illegal entry. To make sure, he went round the manse a second time. As he passed a water butt, raised two feet above the ground, it toppled over, and drenched him. No thought of the cause worried his mind while he divested himself of his clerical garb in the bedroom, and flung the dripping garments down the stairs, calling to the maid to dry them. For the rest of the day he sat by the fire sneezing, his flesh quivering. That night he ordered the cook to have the maid get two round stones, heat them in the oven, wrap each in a flannel satchel, and put them in his bed. In spite of the warmth of the stones, his back felt cold all through the night.

The maid was the next to be pestered. When she went to heat the stones on the following evening, she could not find them, though the flannel satchels were there. She went to the beach to get two more. Having found one suitable, she placed it above the beach, and sought another. Almost all the stones on the beach were small pebbles, but she found one that would do, and carried it up, intending to pick up the first. But it was gone. She dropped the second, and looked all around. A rattling startled her, and she saw the second stone roll down over the pebbles and go plump into the sea.

'Mercy me!' she exclaimed. 'Something will not let me take big stones. I'll take six smaller ones.'

She did so, carrying them in her apron, and she put them in the oven. When they were hot, she put them in the satchels, and put these in the minister's bed.

Mr McVicar went upstairs after his wife had gone to bed. His cold was some better, and he was looking forward to the comfort of heat on his back and chest. He climbed in beside his wife into a warm bed, reached down to get the

satchels, and put one on his back and the other on his chest.
Warm and comfortable, he was just about dropping off to
sleep, when he gave a gasp. Both satchels not only had
turned icy cold, but also one felt as if things were moving
inside it. Up he jumped.

'What's the matter, Patrick?' asked his alarmed wife.

'The matter! Light the lamp.'

Mrs McVicar did so. The minister pulled out both satchels, and both of them wriggled. He dropped them on the floor. His wife picked one up and undid the cord. She held it upside down. Three young coalfish dropped out and wriggled on the carpet. The McVicars gazed in horror. Mrs McVicar recovered, opened the window, and threw the other satchel out. Then she rang for the maid, who came up and looked in surprise at her employers in their voluminous night shirts.

'Jeannie, look what you put in your master's flannels.'

Jeannie looked at the fish with popping eyes.

'I never did. I put in three stones. Where would I get the cuithes?'

'Go down and get the other satchel from outside the window. Take it up, and bring cook with you.'

Jeannie did so, and soon returned with old Mrs Norquoy, the cook. Sure enough, when the satchel was gingerly opened as it wriggled, three cuithes were in it.

'Mrs Norquoy,' said Mrs McVicar, 'could anyone have put fish in these instead of the stones Jeannie says she put?'

'No,' said the cook. Nobody could have done so. I saw her put the stones in with my own eyes.'

The four looked at one another in consternation. A slithering attracted their attention. Two satchels lay on the floor, but the fish were gone.

'I know, sir. I know,' said the cook brightly. 'That's the work of a hogboon.'

'A hogboon!' exclaimed the McVicars simultaneously.

'Aye, a bogle. He'll have been asleep in the mound for long, and now he's up to his tricks again.'

'Have you seen . . . whatever it is?' asked Mrs McVicar.

'You don't see them, ma'am. Never. They just pester from nowhere.'

'They must be sent by Satan to pester me in my good work,' said the minister. 'What am I to do?'

'There's only one thing,' said the cook slowly. 'Put a curse on him. Tell him to be off.'

The minister drew himself up. 'Hog . . .' he shouted. 'What did you call it, cook?'

'Hogboon, sir. Hogboon!'

'Hogboon,' boomed the minister, 'you limb of Satan, go back to where you belong. Back, Hogboon, back to Hell, you offspring of Beelzebub.'

A slithering noise was heard, and then silence.

'That's done for him,' said the cook. 'He'll not dare pester you again.'

She and the maid went away. Mrs McVicar went back to bed. The minister blew out the lamp, and as he padded to the bed he stepped on the slimy spot where the fish had fallen. He shivered, and dived under the bedclothes.

In spite of his sufferings, Mr McVicar rose in the morning, his cold better, and pleased with the effect of his curse. As days went by and no hogboon tormented him he remarked to his wife: 'The imp has gone where I commanded him to go.'

Mr McVicar was right, though not in the way he understood. Robbie Cursitter knew that the hogboon was back in the mound at Hell, but it was a changed creature. Mrs Cursitter found her eggs gathered; Robbie found his grain winnowed and later it was flailed for him. His wife found her empty waterpail full, and peats carried in. In their failing days the hogboon was a great boon to them.

Meanwhile, Henry Hay had found it impossible to meet all the minister's demands, and sadly gave up Paradise, and took service with a big farmer. As other crofters knew why Henry had given up, no one wanted to take the place. At last Mr McVicar got Jim Cursitter to take it and its duties for a fixed rent in cash, the minister getting another crofter to work his acres, and pay for its props in kind. A year passed, and Mr McVicar was appointed to a church outside the island, somewhere in Fife, and a young Mr Ritch was appointed to St Colms.

When the old Cursitters died, Mr Ritch restored the

former Helye to its original size, giving Jim Cursitter the tenancy. As his father's buildings were in disrepair, Jim took the roof off the house, and replaced his thatch roof with the flag-stone roof of Hell, and in the years following removed all the stones from Hell and Paradise. The hogboon did not live on in the memories of the generations that followed. The wiser sons of the fathers regarded all old legends as superstitions. But when the writer was a boy, he heard his elders speak of the houses of Hell and Paradise, and Purgatory was then standing, and still stands today. Shortly after World War I, a James Cursitter of Purgatory appeared before the Crofters' Commission that was enquiring into rents and other things. Cursitter was asked by the chairman if he was the man who took the roof off Hell and put it on Purgatory.

W.T.C.

THE SEA FOLK

The Storm Child

In storm she came, and in storm she went. Washed up on the ness many, many years ago, the Storm Child was plucked from a rock pool by Jamie Dass, the crofter. The gale that cast her ashore had, in the same night, scattered the wreckage of a great Indiaman along the island skerries; Jamie Dass lost a chance at some good driftwood while he took the foundling home to his wife.

Nothing was ever discovered about her. No women survived the wreck of the Indiaman; none of the half-dozen men who came ashore knew of there being an infant aboard. And so James and Mary Dass kept the Storm Child.

She was tiny: by her size, perhaps a year old. Mary Dass warmed her and coaxed her to drink a little milk. Then she carefully cut away the thin, soaked, greenish scraps like tatters of seaweed that clung to the fragile limbs. All the while the babe skirled tearlessly, high and thin like a seagull's wail. But Mary persevered, cleaning away the ragged wisps until only a fine dark line remained down each leg from hip to heel. These she could not wash away, so like a wise woman – or a fool – she said nothing about them. Wrapping the babe in a bit of linen cloth, she rocked it gently and it slept. In a few days it was thriving, a silent little creature who never cried.

They called her Sibilla. Their only child, a grown man by now, lived away from the island, and Mary Dass was glad to have this one for company. Not much company, said the

neighbours: indeed, Sibilla did not speak until she was near
ten years old by Mary's reckoning. She was a delicate-
looking girl, pale and thin, with long lank fair hair. Most of
the time she was gentle and biddable, though absent-
minded.

She did little enough to help her foster parents. She
would feed the hens and tend the cow, or gather a little
driftwood if Mary or Jamie were with her. Left to herself
on the sands, she was forgetful, returning, most likely, with
only a handful of shells. She shrank and shuddered away
from the fire and never learned to cook. But Mary made
much of her and would hear no word against her.

Others looked askance at Sibilla. Why, they asked, did
she not play with other children? Why did she slip away
whenever possible from her foster mother on the way to
kirk? And hide from the minister? They recalled that her
christening had put her into convulsions. . . . It was uncanny too, the way she listened by the hour to the murmur
of a large, spotted cowrie shell that some earlier ocean-
going Dass had brought home.

'What do you hear, Sibilla?' said Mary casually one day

when the child had laid the shell down for a moment. Surprisingly, Sibilla answered.

'My sea,' she said clearly in a sweet, caressing voice. She picked up the cowrie again, and her clear, light blue eyes once more gazed vacantly past her foster mother.

Delighted and amazed, Mary poured forth a torrent of questions and exclamations. But Sibilla did not reply. Pressed, she withdrew into a corner, her downcast eyes greenish and evasive in the shadow.

Mary did not give up.

'You can go down to the shore and hear the sea, Sibilla,' she said another day. 'You do not need the shell to listen to the sea.'

Sibilla shook her head. '*My* sea,' she said again, and ran her delicate hand over the spotted curves of the cowrie.

'What does the whelk say?' asked Mary, thinking to humour her. Sibilla did not reply. She never listened to the murmur of the whelk.

Having found that her foster child could talk, Mary Dass tried in vain to provoke further speech. Sibilla said nothing more for months. She was growing fast, and growing very pretty. Her limp fine hair had lost its faint greenish sheen and glinted gold in the sunlight. The pallor of her skin was now delicately rose-tinted, her thin face rounding out.

When by Mary's reckoning Sibilla was about twelve, one of the island families moved away. Among the dispersed contents of their cottage was a handsome shell, a nautilus, all spiral coils and pink pearly mouth. Thinking to please Sibilla, James Dass brought it home and put it into her hands. The colour ran up into her face, and her blue eyes came suddenly to life. She sat down, entranced, and raised it to her ear.

'What do you hear, lassie?' asked James, who had doubted Mary's account of Sibilla's speech.

'*My* sea!' said Sibilla. 'My sea calling.'

'There, James!' said Mary triumphantly. She turned to Sibilla. 'What does it say?'

'It says *listen*,' replied Sibilla.

And she spoke no more, shrinking away unhappily when questioned.

Day after day thereafter she listened intently to the new shell, often with signs of pleasure. Then came an equinoctial gale with high wind and rain squalls alternating with sun. All day Sibilla moved restlessly about the cottage from window to door, careless with her little tasks. Towards evening, Mary chided her gently.

'Put the shell up, Sibilla. You must do your work first.'

But the girl clutched the nautilus fiercely and backed away. Her eyes gleamed a cold blue-green, and her hair seemed to crackle and glint of itself.

'No,' she cried. 'No!'

'Sibilla!' said her foster-mother anxiously, 'What is wrong? What do you hear?'

The Storm Child had raised the shell and was listening with parted lips. Her eyes blazed eerily with lambent fire.

'My sisters!' she cried shrilly. 'My sisters are calling! Now I can find the way!'

Flinging off her woollen shawl and tearing at the neck of her shift, she whirled and ran out into the gale, moving clumsily in her long homespun skirt. Mary followed as fast as her stiff limbs permitted. Sibilla made for the ness where the water was breaking white. She paused at the edge of the rocks to shed her shift and drop her heavy skirt. Then, golden hair flying, she ran swiftly, her back and shoulders gleaming white in a momentary ray of sunlight. From the waist down, flowing green folds rippled around her as she fled across the rocks. At the edge, she bent, and swept the green folds close about her knees. They clung; they shimmered—pearl and silver and rose like the sides of a fresh-caught salmon. Then she flung her arms over her head and cried out sweet and shrill, and a great foaming breaker rolled in and swept her away.

At the edge of the sand lay the skirt and shift, and the broken, pearl-lined nautilus shell.

M.N.C.

Johnie Croy of Volyar and the Mermaid

Long ago, Johnie Croy of Volyar was the bravest, boldest and bonniest man in all the broken isles of Orkney. Many a fair lass cast longing glances at Johnie, but never a one did he care for. Now it happened one day that Johnie went to seek driftwood on the shore on the west side of Sanday. The tide was out, and he was threading his way through the big boulders under the crags. Suddenly he heard the most lovely voice singing a strange sweet tune. For a moment he stood dumbfounded with the beauty of the music. It came from the other side of a big point of the crag, and when Johnie peeped around it, he saw a wonderful sight.

On a weed-covered rock sat a mermaid, combing her long hair. Like brightest gold it shone. and flowed down over her white shoulders like sunshine over snow. A silvery, glistening petticoat hung down from her waist, the train of it folded together so that it lay behind her like the tail of a fish. And all the while she combed, she sang her bewitching song.

Johnie Croy was overcome with love of this beautiful creature. She sat with her back to the sea, and he got down and crept quietly among the boulders to get between her and the water. Every glance he cast at her over the stones made his heart burn with love. Quietly as a mouse he crept up, coming within a few feet of her. Still she combed, and still she sang.

Then Johnie sprang forward, flung his arms around her, and kissed her. She leaped to her feet (for two pretty white feet she had under the silvery petticoats). She gave Johnie a wallop with her tail that flung him flat on the rocks, and, gathering the shimmering train of it over her arm, she ran down to the sea. As Johnie scrambled to his feet, he spied the sea maid's golden comb on the sand. She was out in the water now, staring at him with all her eyes, angry at being so rudely kissed, yet with love growing fast in her heart. For only if she can take a mortal lover does the mermaid keep her youth and beauty.

Johnie held up the golden comb and cried, 'Thanks to thee, my bonny lass, for this love-token!'

The mermaid gave a bitter cry. 'Alas, alas! My golden comb! Oh, give me back my golden comb! To lose it will shame me before all my people! Oh, give me back my golden comb!'

'No, no, my sweet!' says Johnie. 'Come you and live on land with me, for never can I love another.'

'Not so,' replied the mermaid. 'I cannot live in your cold land. I cannot bide your black rain and your white snow. And your hot sun and smoky fires would wizen me up in a week. Come with me, my bonny lad. I'll make you a chief among the Fin Folk. Come away, come away with me.'

'No, no,' said Johnie. 'You cannot entice me – I was not born yesterday. But come you to my stately house at Volyar. There I have plenty of gear; I have cows and sheep. I will make you mistress of all my store. Never shall you want, my darling, for what I can give you.'

But the mermaid shook her head and replied,

'Come, come now with me, my bonnie man. I will set you in a crystal palace under the sea. There the sunbeams never blind, there the winds do not blow, and the raindrops never fall. Oh, come away with me, and be my love, and we shall both be happy as the day is long.'

'It is for the lass to follow the lad,' said Johnie Croy. 'Just come away and bide with me, my darling Gem-de-Lovely.'

So there they stood, each tempting the other. And the

longer they gazed, the better they loved. But at last Gem-de-Lovely saw folk coming far away. Bidding Johnie farewell, she swam out to sea, singing mournfully, 'Alas, alas! My golden comb! Alas, my bonnie man!' And Johnie watched her go, her golden locks shining over her white shoulders like sunbeams glinting over sea-foam.

Then he went home with a sore heart, carrying the golden comb. His mother was a Spae-Wife, a wise old woman, and Johnie Croy told her all his tale and asked her advice.

'Great fool that you are!' said his mother. 'To fall in love with a sea maid where any land lass would be glad of you! But men will be fools all the world over. To bring this sea wife to you, you must keep her comb well hidden; it is her dearest treasure. Keep it, and you have power over her. Now be wise, my son; take my advice. Cast the comb into the sea, and forget her. The folk of the sea are not of God's people.'

But Johnie Croy could not do that.

'Then,' said Grannie Croy, 'she may make a bright summer for you, but it will end in a woeful winter. I see you will ride your own road, though you sink in the quagmire at its end. One I could save – I would it were you, my son. But what will be, will be.'

Well, Johnie went about his work like one bewitched, thinking all the while of his Gem-de-Lovely. But he put the Comb up safely for all that.

Then came a night when he could not sleep for tossing about and thinking of his love. Towards morning he dozed, and at day-break he was wakened by beautiful music. He lay awhile as if enchanted: it was the voice that he had last heard at the shore. Gem-de-Lovely was sitting at the foot of the bed, the most beautiful being that ever gladdened a man's eyes. Her face was so fair, her hair so gleaming, and her dress so splendid that Johnie took her for a vision and tried to say a prayer. But never a word of a prayer came to his lips.

'My bonnie man,' said the mermaid, 'I'm come to ask

again for my golden comb. I'm come to see if you will live with me in my crystal palace under the waves.'

'No,' said Johnie. 'No, my sweet! That I cannot do. But unless you bide with me now and be my loving wife, my heart will break.'

'I will make you a fair offer,' said Gem-de-Lovely. 'I will be your wife. I will live here with you for seven years, if you will swear to come with me and all that's mine, to see my own folk at the end of that time.'

With that, Johnie jumped out of bed, fell on his knees before her, and swore to keep the bargain.

And so they were married. Gem-de-Lovely shivered and shook as they came to the church, and stuffed her hair in her ears as the priest prayed. But folks soon forgot that, for a bonnier bride was never seen in Orkney. Her face was as lovely as the dawn; her dress shone with silver and gold; and every pearl in her necklace was as big as a cockle shell.

Gem-de-Lovely was a frugal, loving wife to Johnie Croy. She baked the best bread in the island, and brewed the strongest ale. She was the best spinner in all the country-side. For seven years, everything at Volyar was in good order: the sheep and the cattle thrived; the barns were full. All things went merry as a Yuletide from one year to the next. But all good things must end; and the seventh year drew to a close.

Then you may believe there was a stir in making ready for a long sea voyage. Johnie said little, but he thought much. Gem-de-Lovely was brisk and busy, and wore a far-away look. By now, they had seven bonnie bairns, all as strong and well-favoured as their parents. Each of them in turn was weaned in Grannie Croy's little house, and now she had the youngest sleeping in her own room. And what do you think Grannie Croy did on the eve of the day when the seven years ended?

She rose in the midnight, and blew up the ashes in the fire. She made a cross of wire and heated it red-hot in the embers. And she laid the red-hot cross on the bare seat of the babe, he screeching like a demon all the while.

In the morning when they were fully equipped, Gem-de-Lovely walked down to the boat. And oh! she was a picture. Stately and splendid as a queen in her shining dress with the great pearls gleaming on her neck, she came to the beach. There was her goodman, Johnie Croy. There were her six eldest bairns. There was Grannie Croy, sitting on a stone with the tear in her eye.

Gem-de-Lovely sent up the servants to Grannie Croy's little house to bring the seventh bairn down in his cradle. Back they came, telling her that the four of them could not budge it one inch. A cloud came over her beautiful face. She ran up to the house and tried to move the cradle. Not an inch would it budge. She flung back the blanket to lift the babe out in her arms. But the moment she touched him, she felt a dreadful burning and started back with a wild scream. Down to the beach she went, her head hanging and the tears streaming from her deep blue eyes. And all the while, Grannie Croy sat on the stone with the tears on her cheek and a half-smile on her lips.

As the boat pushed off, they heard Gem-de-Lovely lamenting sore. 'Alas, alas, for my bonnie boy! Alas, that I must leave one to live and die on dry land!'

The wind blew; the sail filled. The boat turned to the west and swiftly disappeared. Johnie Croy and his fair wife and their six eldest bairns were never more seen in Orkney. But Grannie Croy nursed up the babe that was left, and she named him Corsa Croy (Croy of the Cross). He grew up the bravest, the boldest and the bonniest man in the islands. When his grandmother died, Corsa Croy took to the sword. Far over seas he went on crusade to fight the Pagans in the Holy Land. And men said that enemies fell before his blade like thistles to the reaping-hook. Corsa Croy became rich and famous. He married a great jarl's daughter and settled in the south country. He and his wife had many bairns and long life and happiness, for the descendants of the sea-folk are always handsome and always lucky.

W.T.C.

A Night at a Tavern in Trondheim

Mansie Mowat from the islands was out of luck that year. First there had been the loss of his fishing net and with it the hope of a good season's fishing. Then he sailed with a vessel plying to Norway, and fell ill there on his second voyage. By the time he was fit to leave, none of his fellow Orcadians were in port, nor could he find an Orkney ship at anchor, for it was late in the season. At dusk, very discouraged, he turned away from the harbour and began to trudge back to his poor lodging house. He knew that his money could not last long and wondered what would happen if he fell ill again.

Then a deep voice hailed him by name.

'Mansie Mowat of Corstain! And how is it with thee, Mansie?'

'I've had it better,' admitted Mansie, wondering who the man was. Little could be seen in the shadows save that he was tall and broad and well clad in heavy sea gear.

'Well, come away and have a cog of ale,' boomed the other, and Mansie accepted. The sea fog was creeping in from the water, and the chill struck to his bones. It is a lonely thing to be ill in a strange land.

Meanwhile the big man had taken a turning or two off the High Street, always to the left. They stopped outside a closed dark house. He knocked, and an old woman let them in. They stepped into a narrow stone passage leading to a long room at the back. Singing and laughter and the welcome noises of a comfortable tavern came to their ears.

Once in the room, Mansie saw by the light of the crusie lamps a well-sanded floor, and long tables and benches nearly filling the room. Two or three young girls and the old woman who had answered the door were serving a number of customers, and others entered behind Mansie.

His companion called for a cog of ale, heated.

'You're no' looking as well as you were at the fishing last summer, Mansie,' he remarked.

Mansie explained that he had just risen from a sickbed.

'Aye, aye!' said the other. 'Bring a bannock and something to go with it,' he added to the serving girl, a plump, brown-eyed lass with long dark hair and a shy smile.

Men came and went in the room with casual greetings. Mansie, who was beginning to feel the effects of his hot ale before he had drunk a quarter of it, thought they all had the same sort of look. All were stout, muscular, round-headed fellows, all well clad with sealskin waistcoats and good sea boots. The food arrived – cheese and bannock and pickled herring done in the Norse fashion – all served on a wooden trencher without knife or fork. Mansie found he was hungry and ate heartily.

Then a singer arose at the far end of the room. Several voices called suggestions to him, and after a minute or two he began a long sentimental ballad. The plaintive tune, was half familiar to Mansie, who caught verses here and there.

> *. . . An' de goodman say*
> *Come awey, awey,*
> *An' live on de land wi' me.*
>
> *Me house is warm*
> *From de cold an' storm,*
> *An' me door is open to thee.*
>
> *An' de sea maid know*
> *Dat she kinno go*
> *In de woolen shift an' de leather shoe*
>
> *An' on land she stay . . .*

After every three or four verses came a chorus in which most of the customers joined heartily,

> *But de Selkie Wyf loved de selkie life –*
> *An' back she come to de sea!*

It went on and on, and Mansie looked around him curiously. But his host leaned forward and said,

'Now, Mansie what's to be done with thee?'

'Are thoo at sea theeself?' asked Mansie hopefully.

'Yes – in a wey of speaking,' replied the other. 'But I'm bound for the Faroes in the morning, and that's little good to you, Mansie,' he added with his rumbling laugh.

'True,' admitted Mansie disconsolately.

'So I think we'll just put thee aboard the German barque that's leaving at first light. She'll be calling in at Kirkwall.'

And before Mansie could speak, he shouted for another song and another two cogs of ale, and got up and went about the room speaking to men at the different tables.

Mansie sat drinking his second cog of ale and half dozing. It seemed to him that he had seen these companions of his before – they were familiar and yet not known to him by name. And the incomers looked curiously at him before joining the company. A new song was in progress – a soft crooning like a lullaby . . .

Some time later the big man shook him roughly.

'Time to move,' he said. 'The barque is readying.'

And they were out in the street before Mansie, only half awake, realized that the room was silent and nearly empty. Two or three turns to the left, and they were down at the harbour in no time. The German barque was there, and Mansie's companion halted at the edge of the pier. Mansie began to utter his stumbling thanks, but the big man laughed.

'No, no,' he said. 'I owe thee something in compensation for the net.'

'*You* owe me?' said Mansie, dazed. 'The net that the seal . . . ?'

'Aye,' said the other. 'It were an accident, Mansie, but

a net's a lot to a poor man. Though you gave me a right handy blow, Mansie, with that boat-hook o' thine!'

And pushing back his sealskin sea-cap, he showed a long scar running across the brown, close-cropped scalp above the right eye.

'But that's all in the day's work!' he added cheerfully, with a friendly blow on the back and a heave that sent Mansie stumbling up the gangway. On board, he found he was expected, and that his passage was paid to Kirkwall.

Meanwhile the burly companion of the night had disappeared. Mansie's memories of him were hazy; but he recalled quite clearly that his boat-hook had caught the great seal that had ruined the net above its right eye.

W.T.C.

One Spared to the Sea

It is many years now since Willie Westness of Over-the-Watter was digging lugworms for bait in the little sandy bay on the east side of Elsness. By the time his pail was full, the tide had not yet turned. The trink was still safe to cross, and he decided to look for driftwood farther along the shore. Then it was that he heard the cry from the rocks – a moan like that of a woman in pain swelling into a loud, strange sound and dying into a sort of sob. It seemed to come from the geo, a little inlet hidden behind the rocks and covered at high tide. Out in the deep water a big seal had raised its head and was listening and watching intently.

Willie moved quietly towards the geo. Coming around the rocks that had hidden it, he saw, lying on the shelving stone, another big seal. Beside her was a newborn pup. As the mother began to move, he ran down over the rocks. The seal flopped into the water, but the pup lay helpless at his feet. It squirmed as he picked it up, and then pressed against him and nuzzled at his hand.

I'll take it home for the bairn, thought Willie, and keep it in the small loch at Over-the-Watter.

At the edge of the rocks the mother seal splashed and sobbed in distress. When he glanced up, she was pulling herself clumsily back out of the water to lie moaning at the edge, her round eyes full of tears. The pup too gazed at him with soft blurred brown eyes, and nosed at his sleeve. Its little sleek round head was like a child's . . .

'Ach, selkie, take thee bairn and be gone wi' ye!' said Willie Westness aloud. He put the pup down close to the water's edge and watched the seal come to it. Then he collected his pail of lugworms and trudged back over the trink where the tide was just beginning to run.

Nine years afterwards, Willie Westness had a family of four. One fine day the three youngest went wading for cockles at the little sandy bay. They knew well enough that they should not cross the trink, where the water swept in

so fast and deep on the high tide. But they had heard their
father say that the cockles were better there than in the
large bay itself, and after a little argument among themselves, they crossed over.

'We won't stay long,' said Johnny, the eldest.

'We'll hurry back,' agreed his sister, Jeanie.

The cockles were plentiful, and they went on gathering.
When the pail was nearly full, they turned towards home.

The tide was flowing fast. The trink had widened.

'Hurry!' said Johnny.

But for all that he and Jeanie pulled and scolded, little Tam's fat legs could not be hurried over the rocks. Every minute the water deepened. When it was about their ankles, the two younger began to cry, clinging together and pressing back into a corner of the rocks. Johnny stood further out, watching the waves rising and shouting with all his might. But no one appeared across the trink to help them, and the water rose steadily.

Then they heard a soft voice singing almost beside them. Two people had come up behind them – two grey-cloaked women that they did not know.

'Come away, bairns,' said the elder. She had a plump, friendly face and round brown eyes. 'Come away. It will soon be too late.'

She took little Tam and Jeanie by the hands and led them straight into the water that was now up to their knees where they stood. Up to their middles it rose, and before they had crossed the trink, up to their necks. But held in her firm, warm grasp they kept their footing and found themselves in safety on the far side. Looking back, they saw their brother coming hand-in-hand with the smaller, slimmer woman. Her other hand held the bucket of cockles, balancing it on her head.

'All's well,' said the older woman cheerfully, and the younger smiled shyly and looked at them kindly from her brown eyes.

'Now take thee father a word from me,' said the elder. 'Remember now, say to thee father, Willie Westness, to mind a day when he digged lugworm at the geo, nine summers gone. And say to him that one spared to the sea is three spared to the land.'

And she bade them repeat the message till it was right: 'One spared to the sea is three spared to the land.'

'Now run away home, bairns,' she said. 'And dunno pass the trink again – I came for once only. Run away home!' And she gave them a little push.

Obediently they ran. And when they looked back from the foreshore, the tide was pouring through the trink and the water was high over the rocks. No grey-cloaked women were in sight, and two seals were swimming towards the point of Elsness.

M.N.C.

'Eyn-Hallow Free'

Eyn-Hallow frank, Eyn-Hallow free,
Eyn-Hallow stands in the middle of the sea
With a roaring roost on every side,
Eyn-Hallow stands in the middle of the tide.
(Old rhyme)

This is the story of how the island of Eyn-Hallow (meaning Holy Isle, or some say, Last-hallowed) was taken from the Fin Folk and came to be part of the Orkneys.

The goodman of Thorodale in Evie married a wife and she bore him three sons. After her death, he married another, the bonniest lass in Evie, and dearly Thorodale loved her. One day he and his bonny wife were down in the ebb. Thorodale sat on a rock to tie his shoe-string, turning his back to his wife who was nearer the sea. Suddenly she began to scream. Thorodale turned and saw a tall dark man dragging her towards a boat. He rushed down and waded into the sea, but the dark man had the young woman in the boat and pulled out before Thorodale could reach them. Long before he got to his own boat, the Fin Man was out of sight. For by their sorcery, the Fin Folk can make their vessels invisible, propelling them more swiftly than a bird in flight.

Now Thorodale was not the man to take such a blow quietly. There in the ebb he knelt down and he swore that, living or dead, he would be revenged on the Fin Folk. Many a long night and day he thought on his vengeance, but no way could he see. Then one day he was fishing in the sound between Ronsay and Evie. No Eyn-Hallow could be seen there then. As part of the Fin Folk's summer home, their Hilda-Land, it was often hidden below the waves, and it was always invisible to human eyes. Well, Thorodale lay fishing at slack tide near the middle of the sound, when he heard a female voice singing. It was that of his lost wife, though he could not see her.

'Goodman, grieve no more for me,'

she sang prettily,

> *'For me again you'll never see;*
> *If you would have of vengeance joy –*
> *Go ask the wise Spae-Wife of Hoy!'*

Thorodale went on shore, took his staff in his hand, took his silver in a stocking, and set off to the island of Hoy. What passed between him and the wise woman, I do not know, but certainly she told him how to get the power of seeing Hilda-Land. She told him, too, how he was to act when he saw any of those hidden isles; and she said that nothing could punish the Fin Folk more than taking any part of their Hilda-Land from them.

And so Thorodale went home. For nine moons, at midnight when the moon was full, he went nine times on his bare knees around the great Odin Stone of Stenness. For nine moons, at full moon, he looked through the hole in the Odin Stone and wished that he might get the power of seeing Hilda-Land. After doing this for nine months on the days when the moon was full, he bought a great quantity of salt. He filled a meal chest with salt, and set three large kaesies (straw baskets) beside it. His three sons were now well-grown young men, and he told them what to do when he gave the word. And he made other preparations too.

One beautiful summer morning just after sunrise, Thorodale looked out on the sea. There in the middle of the sound, lay a pretty little island where never land was seen before. Without taking his eyes off it, he roared out to his three sons in the house,

'Fill the kaesies and hold for the boat!'

Down came the sons, carrying the kaesies of salt, which they set in the boat. The four men jumped in and rowed straight for the new island, but only Thorodale could see it.

In a moment, the boat was surrounded by whales. The three sons wanted to try to drive the whales, but their father knew better.

'Pull for your lives,' he cried, 'and Deil catch the delayer!'

Then a monster of a whale raised its head right in the boat's course, opening a mouth huge enough to swallow men and boat at a single gulp. But Thorodale bade his sons bend to the oars, and he rose to his feet in the bow. Right into the terrible jaws he flung a double handful of salt. In the same moment, the monster vanished. It was only an apparition, a trick of the Fin Men's scorery, and the salt, a consecrated substance, destroyed the evil magic.

The boat was fast nearing Hilda-Land. Two most beautiful mermaids stood waist-deep at the shore, their long golden hair fluttering over their white shoulders. So melodious was their song that it went to the hearts of the rowers, and the young men began to row slowly. But Thorodale, without turning his head or taking his eyes off the island, kicked the two sons nearest him, and the boys mended their stroke. Then he cried to the mermaids,

'Begone, you unholy limmers! Here's your warning!'

And he threw a cross made of twisted tangles on each of them. Then the mermaids plunged under the sea with pitiful shrieks, and the boat touched the enchanted shore.

There on the beach stood a huge and horrible monster. Its tusks were as long as a man's two arms; its feet as broad as quern-stones. Its eyes blazed, its mouth spat fire. But Thorodale leaped boldly on to the land, flinging a handful of salt between the monster's glaring eyes. With a terrible growl, it too disappeared.

In its place there stood before him a tall and mighty man, dark, scowling, with a drawn sword in his hand.

'Go back!' he roared. 'Go back, you human thieves, you that come to rob the Fin Folk's land! Begone! Or by my father's head, I'll defile Hilda-Land with your nasty blood!'

When the three sons heard that, they trembled and said, 'Come home, Dad, come home!'

And the big Fin Man made a sudden thrust at Thorodale's breast. But Thorodale sprang aside, and flung a cross in his face. It was made of the sticky grass called 'cloggirs', and when it touched the dark skin, it clung. And it would not fall off! Then the dark man turned and fled, roaring as he ran with pain and grief and fury. And Thorodale knew him for the very Fin Man that had dragged his young wife away from the beach. You must understand that the Fin Man was afraid to pull the cross from his face because to touch it with his hand would have caused him more pain. The blessed symbols are agony to those under the Devil's rule.

Then Thorodale cried to his sons who still sat dumbfounded in the boat,

'Come out of that you duffers! Bring the salt ashore!'

The three sons came on shore, each carrying his big kaesie of salt. And their father lined them up and bade them walk abreast around the island, each scattering salt as he went. When they began sowing the salt, there arose a terrible rumpus among the Fin Folk and their beasts. Out of the houses and byres and down to the sea they all ran, helter-skelter like a flock of sheep with mad dogs at their heels. The Fin Men roared, the mermaids screamed, and the cattle bellowed so that it was awful to hear them. The end of it was that every last mother's son of them and every hair of their beasts took to the sea, never again to set foot on the island. Their homes and steadings, their crops too, disappeared.

Thorodale cut nine crosses on the turf of the island, and his three sons went three times around it sowing their salt, nine rings of salt in all. And so the Fin Folk's Hilda-Land was cleared of all enchantment and lay bare and empty and clean to the sight of man and heaven. Then it was called Eyn-Hallow, the Holy Isle (or the Last-hallowed), and a church was raised there.

That is how the goodman of Thorodale took revenge on the Fin Folk.

W.T.C.

'A Close Tongue
Keeps a Safe Head'

Tam Scott of Sanday was as clever a boatman as ever set foot on the tulfer – that is, until misfortune befell him. One fall when he had taken a number of Sanday folk to the Lammas Fair in Kirkwall, he was going up and down through the fair, greeting acquaintances. Up comes a big, tall man with a dark-bearded face.

'The top of the day to you,' says the stranger.

'As much to you,' says Tam, who was a friendly, talkative sort. 'But I'm a liar if I said I know who speaks to me.'

'Never mind,' says the other. 'Will you take a cow of mine to one of the north isles? I'll pay double freight for taking you away so soon from the fair.'

'That I will!' says Tam, for he was not the boy to stick at a bargain when he saw the butter on his own side of the bread.

By the time he got to the shore and made the boat ready, he saw the big dark man coming down leading his cow. When he came to the edge of the water, the stranger lifted the cow in his arms as if she had been a sheep, and set her down in the boat.

'By my soul, goodman, you've not been last in line when strength was given out!' cried Tam. But never a word said the stranger.

When they got under way, Tam asked, 'Where are we to steer for?'

'East of Shapinsay,' says his passenger.

When at Shapinsay, Tam asked, 'Where now?'

'East of Stronsay,' says the man.

When they were off Mill Bay in Stronsay, Tam said, 'You'll be for landing here?'

'East of Sanday,' rumbled the other.

Now Tam Scott liked to talk, and as they sailed along, he had tried hard to engage the passenger in friendly chat. But to every remark he made, the man only replied gruffly,

'A close tongue keeps a safe head.'

At last it dawned on Tam's mind that he had an uncanny freight on board, and he fell silent for a while. But as they sailed on through the east sea, he saw rising ahead a dense fog bank, and he said,

'I make no doubt here we're coming into mist.'

The stranger muttered grumpily. 'A close tongue keeps a safe head.'

'Faith,' says Tam, 'that may be true; but a close mist will not be very safe for you and me.'

For the first time the passenger smiled, a sort of sulky

smile to himself. Tam thought it did not improve his dark, lowering face.

But now the bank of mist ahead was shining like a cloud at sunset. Then it slowly rolled up, and Tam saw lying ahead under it a most beautiful island that he did not know. Men and women were walking about; cattle fed in the green pastures; and the yellow cornfields were ripe for harvest. Tam stared with all his eyes at the lovely land, and the dark-visaged stranger sprang aft.

'I must blindfold you for a little while,' he said. 'Do what you are told and no harm shall come of it.'

Tam thought it wiser to submit, and the man blindfolded him with his own neckerchief. In a few minutes the boat grounded on a gravelly beach. He heard many men's voices speaking to his passenger. And he heard too the loveliest music that ever struck his ears. It was the sweet, melodious voices of mermaids singing on the shore. By tipping his head sideways, he could just catch a glimpse of them from the corner of his eye where the blindfold was a little thin. Then the dark-faced man called out roughly,

'You idle limmers! If you think to charm this man you are wasting your time. He has a wife and bairns of his own in Sanday Isle.'

As he spoke, the music changed to a sad, wailing song that brought the tears to Tam's eyes.

Meanwhile the cow was lifted out, and a big bag of money laid at Tam's feet in the stern. The men shoved the boat off. And what do you think? The graceless wretches turned it *against the sun*, as Fin Men always do. As they pushed it off, one of them cried,

'Keep the starboard end of the fore-thaft bearing on the Brae of Warsater, and you'll soon make land.'

When Tam felt the boat under way, he tore off the bandage, but he could see nothing all around save the thick mist. He soon sailed out of it, leaving it lying astern in a great cloud. Then he saw the Brae of Warsater bearing on the starboard bow, and sailed home. On opening his bag of money, he found he was well paid, but all in copper coins.

For, you see, the Fin Men love silver far too well to part with white money.

Now a twelvemonth later, Tam Scott was again at Lammas Fair in Kirkwall. Many a time afterwards he wished that he had lain in bed that day: but what must be, must be. It was the third day of the market, and Tam, as usual, was walking up and down speaking to acquaintances, and taking a cog of ale once in a while with a friend. Then whom should he spy but the same big, tall, dark-faced man that gave him the freight the year before? In his own free way, Tam ran up and said,

'How is all with you, goodman? So might I thrive as I am happy to see you! Come an' take a cog of ale with me! And how have you been since I last saw you?'

'Did you ever see me?' said the Fin Man, and O, the ugly look on his dark face! As he spoke he took out what Tam thought was a snuff-box. He opened the box, and he blew some of what was in it right into Tam's eyes, saying,

'Ye shall never have to say that ye saw me again!'

And from that moment, poor Tam Scott never again saw a blink of the sweet light with his two eyes. You see, we should not make over-free with folk we do not know: 'A close tongue keeps a safe head.'

W.T.C.

# The Talisman Knife

Long ago before the sea had eaten in and the blowing sand covered its once-fertile fields, the farm of Langtas extended green across the Catasands to meet the cultivated fields of Erraby, both dating back to the early Norse settlements. In Langtas lived old Alec Dearness, his wife, Mary Jean, his one bonny daughter, Lily, and his three sons, Ned, Bob and Davie. They lived comfortably for their times, the whole family helping with the farm work, as Alec did much fishing besides his farming. In the evenings he often spoke of the strange notions his fishing partner, John Muir, held. He laughed as he told how once, when they had rounded Tresness as a fog was clearing, John had declared that he could see an island far out from Erraby shining in the sunlight. A down-to-earth man was old Alec, with no belief in the ancient stories his neighbours told sitting around their fires in the long winter evenings.

One day when Alec was at home, the three boys set out to gather driftwood around the point of Tresness. Lily decided to go raking cockles at Erraby, where the boys would join her later, and all come back together. So she set off with pail and rake, and the boys worked their way slowly around the point. When they came to the cockle beds, they found the rake and the half-filled pail of cockles, but Lily had disappeared. Long they searched and loud they called, but no trace of their sister was ever found, and at last the family mourned her as dead. Her mother, Mary Jean, died the next year, and then old

Alec Dearness was a lonely man indeed when his sons were at sea.

Five years later he was fishing one morning early off Erraby with Davie, his youngest son. A heavy fog came down suddenly and the two were not sure of their bearings. After a time they heard waves on a beach, and began watching anxiously for the shore. When the fog lifted a little, they found themselves in a bay that they did not recognize. Seeing a boat house near by, they decided to go ashore and ask where they were. They made the boat fast, then followed a path leading up from the ebb to a gate in a well-built stone wall. The mist was clearing fast and they saw ahead a fine white stone house in a garden, and other buildings at the back of it. As they came up, an animal lying across the doorstep slipped silently aside, and young Davie saw with surprise that it was an otter. His father, who had not noticed, was knocking at the door. The young woman who answered started back with a wild shriek, then, bursting into tears, she flung her arms around old Alec and drew him inside.

'Father!' she cried, 'I thought never to see thee again!'

The old man was overcome, and Lily helped him to a seat by the fire. Then she greeted her brother, whom she had not at first recognized, with affection, and called out her two children who were playing in the next room. The old man looked anxiously at them, and, beginning to recover, tried to coax them to him. Meanwhile Davie gazed curiously around the room. Fine carved wooden chests stood along the walls; silver cups gleamed on the mantel-shelf; through the window he caught a glimpse of a bluish-roan cow grazing in a pasture near by.

'What is this place?' he demanded of his sister.

'This is Heather-Bleather,' said Lily quietly, and the hairs rose on the back of Davie's neck.

'How did you get here?' he whispered hoarsely.

'Ask no questions,' replied his sister in the same low

voice. 'You are welcome – you will come to no harm now. – but ask no questions.'

Before she had finished speaking there was a sound outside, and two strange figures appeared in the doorway. One discarded a sealskin as he entered; the other began unwinding the bale of simmons in which he had wrapped his legs. The otter came in with them and stayed close about their feet. Away from their disguises, the two proved to be big, dark-skinned muscular Fin Men, handsome enough in feature, but with expressionless faces and oddly blank eyes. They were Lily's husband, Dogg, and his brother, Graef. Both greeted the visitors courteously and bade them welcome. Then they all sat down to the good dinner that Lily served, and drank their ale afterwards from the fine silver cups. The whole house was richly furnished, and the farmyard that they saw later was well stocked.

Late in the afternoon, Davie Dearness spoke to his father about leaving. But Lily was grief-stricken and wept and said that she could not bear to lose them again so soon.

'Come with us!' said her brother boldly, but she said that she could not do that: the children were too young to go and she could not leave them.

'But *you* can stay with me!' she said eagerly. 'Stay! There is room for us all here!'

Old Alec would have stayed, for his heart turned to his daughter's children; but Davie was courting a girl at home, and he urged his father to come away before nightfall. Dogg and Graef, their dark opaque eyes fixed on the other three, said not a word of any kind. But Davie had a feeling that a message had passed between them.

'If you will go, then you must,' said the young woman sadly, lifting and clasping her youngest child whom she had named after her father.

'I would come again if I could find thee, my lass,' said old Alec, greatly moved.

'That need not be hard,' said Lily, setting the child down and opening one of the carved chests. 'Take this, Father – see that you keep it safe – and the way will be clear to you every full moon.'

She put into his hand a knife of strange workmanship. It had a fine stone blade bound with silver to a wavy haft of walrus ivory. This was all carved with curious runes inlaid with silver, and the end of the haft was shaped like a serpent's head.

'Keep it safe!' repeated Lily urgently. 'With it you can find the way back to Heather-Bleather when the moon is full.'

The old man grasped the talisman eagerly, and Lily watched him put it safely into his pocket. Then, bidding her and the bairns a cheerful farewell, he followed his son down the path. Turning to look for his father, Davie saw the door close and the great otter lie down once more before it. Dogg and Graef were awaiting them on the beach, and they waded into the water to push off the Dearness boat.

'The line is caught here,' said Graef. 'Where is your knife, Dogg?'

'Up at the house,' said Lily's husband.

'Here – use this . . .' said old Alec without thinking, and he drew his daughter's gift from his pocket. As he held it out, the haft softened and grew slimy, twisting and writhing in his hand. For an instant his grip slackened; wriggling free, the magic blade dived like a fish into the waves and vanished.

In the same moment, Dogg and Graef gave the boat a powerful thrust, turning it against the sun as it floated free, and driving it well off shore. A curtain of fog fell thick behind it and closed around it, cutting off all sight of the island. For a few seconds, Davie and his father heard the waves lapping on the shore of Heather-Bleather. Then they were in deep water, and the mist was brightening ahead. When they came out into daylight, the sun was still high.

Their day with Lily on the enchanted island had been no more than an hour or two.

But lacking the serpent-headed knife, they never found the way back to Heather-Bleather.

W.T.C.

The Blue Cow
from the Sea

Cold-eyed and cold-hearted was Scathorn, the farmer of Koliby. His hand was quick to grasp but slow to give; his voice loud in reproof but silent to friendly greeting. The most work for the least wage was the rule at Koliby, yet Skathorn had silver and to spare. His stacks were well built; his cows the best in the island.

But Scathorn, the goodman of Koliby, was not satisfied. He desired a blue cow from the herds of the Fin Men. For the Fin Folk, in their lands below the sea, live much as men do on land. When the fisherman drew in his net tangled with stalks of barley, he knew it had swept across an underseas field. Sometimes the Fin Men came ashore to buy (and for good money) a beast to replenish their herds. By enchantment they kept it alive, as they did the lasses or lads that they stole away from the land. Sometimes, too, they sent their blue cattle ashore to graze, delighting in robbing the land, were it only of a few bites of good green grass.

These sea cattle were hornless and usually of a strange bluish-roan colour, though a few had sleek black hair which curled up in the wrong direction. Seldom seen, they were very shy, taking to the sea when a human being came in sight. Occasionally, a blue calf was born in a man's herd, and then he knew that the sea kine had pastured with his beasts.

At last Scathorn of Koliby took some silver from his

store and consulted a Spae-Wife. She gave him her advice, and he listened. Then he said,

'Tell me, old woman – will such a beast be mine?'

The wise woman pondered a while with half-shut eyes.

'Aye,' she said. 'It will be yours and it will not be yours. And that you do not seek will be yours, and it will not be yours, and you will seek in vain.'

'Ach! What a jabber!' snapped Scathorn, and he threw down the silver and went home. There he made his plans and waited and watched. Two or three years passed. At last, just before dawn one summer day, he saw a fine blue beast grazing in his seaward field. Quietly he slipped down along the dyke, and ran out between the blue cow and the sea. He flung out the three blue stones that the Spae-Wife had told him to keep always in readiness, and muttered the charm that she had taught him. At once the cow which had been rushing down to the shore fell quiet and began grazing again. Scathorn walked forward with a band to put about its neck to lead it up to his byre. But the blue cow tossed her head and snorted and would neither be led nor driven.

Then a high sweet voice called from the shore,

'Boro, my Boro! Come home to the sea!'

Scathorn turned and saw a young girl standing in the ebb. Long hair flew in the wind, partly hiding her face. She wore a short sealskin mantle and a dull greenish petticoat. She stretched bare arms towards the cow and cried again,

'Boro, my Boro! Come away, come away!'

'Begone!' said Scathorn angrily. 'The beast is mine now!'

'Alas! Alas!' wailed the girl. 'Boro! my Boro! Do not take her away!'

'No cow of yours, you limmer!' replied Scathorn. 'Begone!'

'Oh, give me my cow!' cried the sea maid. 'My father will beat me sorely for losing her!'

'You should have thought of that earlier.' Who is your father?'

'He is Lok Berkimal, the Fin Man,' replied the girl. 'I am Vali, his daughter. I must take the cow home at dawn.'

'You will take her nowhere at dawn,' said Scathorn. 'There is the sun!'

'Alas for my Boro! I shall be beaten!' lamented the girl.

'Am I to give up my sea cow for that?' grumbled Scathorn. 'No, no, lass! You must just take your lumps and watch the beasts better next time.'

And he tried again to drive the blue cow, but it would not go to the byre and it could not go to the sea. And there

they stood all three in the sunlight: the cow tossing its head and lowing, Scathorn shaking with rage, and the Mermaid in the ebb, weeping like a November cloud.

Then Scathorn swore a great oath. 'I wait no longer!' he roared. 'I've seen better-looking lasses scaring crows! But if I can't have the cow without you, I'll take you along!'

And striding into the ebb, he caught the Mermaid by her thin wrist and jerked her roughly up the foreshore.

Weeping and barefooted, she stumbled over the rocks; she touched the blue cow and spoke one low word to her, and they went quietly, all three, over the field and into the byre.

And so it was that Scathorn, the goodman of Koliby, got his blue sea cow, and a sea maid to tend her. And so well did the girl handle the beast that Scathorn set her to work with his own kine. She was a silent girl, the best milkmaid in the island, and the cattle obeyed her as if they were dogs.

Meanwhile the blue cow cast a fine blue heifer calf, and Scathorn was as well pleased as ever man had seen him. When his old housekeeper fell sick, he sent Vali into the kitchen, and there she proved a tidy lass and made fine butter and cheese. The long and the short of it was that Scathorn decided it would profit the farm if he married her, and she made no protest.

When the priest asked her about her parents, she said, 'My mother came from Evie.'

'And the less said about her father, the better,' interrupted Scathorn.

Vali showed no sign of terror when they entered the kirk, and people thought that she had a soul and pitied her. And so they were wed, and within three years there were two bairns about the house. Vali was a good wife and a good mother. It is not so sure that Scathorn was a good husband and a good father. His hand was over-heavy for that.

The first time that he struck her, Vali said,

'That is one paid off.' And she would say no more, but her eyes glowed like a cat's in the dark, and Scathorn swore and went out.

A year or two later, he struck one of the children unjustly, and Vali said, 'That is two paid off.' Scathorn thought she had grown taller as she spoke, but on looking again, she seemed just as usual.

'Two or twenty-two,' he said, 'I will be master here! Do not forget.'

'I do not forget,' she said.

And things went on quietly for another three years. The

blue cattle increased and thrived; the farm was in good order. The children grew tall. They were as silent as their mother, who taught them many things; they were clever with the animals, and the girl was brisk and neat about the house.

Then in harvest time the weather threatened and the work went ill. Scathorn came home early with a scowl on his face, and shouted for his dinner.

'It is not yet ready,' answered Vali.

'And why not, you witch-wife?' shouted her husband, striking at her. But his arm dropped powerless to his side, and Vali stood up straight and tall. She put up her hands and took off the neat white linen mutch that the island wives wore; she laid it and her shawl upon the table, and held out her hands to the children.

'That is three paid off,' she said. 'Three blue stones – three blows – thrice three years!'

And she went outside and stood by the byre and called.

> *Break thy band, Boro!*
> *Bring all of thy skorie,*
> *And follow thou me to the sea!*

At once the big blue cow, who was never far away, came to her. Vali turned without a backwards look and walked down to the sea, her children on either side. Behind her came a long line of the blue cattle of Koliby, led by Boro.

At the edge of the water, she stopped and kissed the children.

'Do as I have told thee,' she said. 'I will not be far away.'

And clad only in her flowing hair and her green petticoats, which now shimmered silver and white and blue, she walked into the water, followed by the blue cattle of the sea, and was gone. Hand in hand, the children went back up the beach and returned to Koliby.

And that was the last that Scathorn of Koliby ever saw of his blue cows and his Mermaid wife. While the children were young, Vali came to see them, always while her husband was away. The boy became a noted healer of animals; the girl, who married and moved to another island, a Spae-Wife. Both of them had, in the island saying, 'more wits than their own'.

As for Scathorn, he was poorer at the end of his life than he had been when he started. Koliby never thrived after Vali returned to the sea; bit by bit the sand crept up on it and the waves ate into the land, and today the fields where the blue cattle grazed lie beneath the water.

M.N.C.

Annie Norn and
The Fin Folk

Pretty Annie Norn lived many years ago on the mainland of Orkney. One evening, she went to the shore at twilight for salt water to boil the supper in. (At that time, salt was scarce and very dear.) But she never returned. Friends and family sought her far and near, searched up and down, along the shores and the sands, by the crags and the geo, through field and furrow. But never a trace of Annie Norn did they find.

'The Trows have taken her,' whispered some.

'The Fin Folk have carried her off,' said others. And all the older people of the island warned their children once again never to venture out on the shore between the lines of high and low water when the sun was down. For the Fairy Folk and the Fin Folk and all kinds of spirits have power when daylight is passing into darkness; and the edges of land and forest and sea are unchancey places at any time.

Three or four years later, an Orkney vessel was coming home from Norway in the fall of the year. One of the sailors, Willie Norn, was a cousin of Annie's. Midway in its voyage, the vessel was caught in a violent tempest, and tossed to and fro for weeks in the North Sea until the crew were thoroughly exhausted. Their food and water was nearly all gone, and they had lost all sense of their bearing, for neither sun nor star was to be seen. Even when the storm abated after many days, a thick mist lay on the sea, and the men could not tell where they were nor what direction they should steer.

Then a small cool wind arose, but instead of making headway when the sails were trimmed, the ship stood still. The men lamented loudly, saying that they were bewitched, and that their end would be to die there in a rotting hulk on this enchanted sea. In the midst of their outcry, a small boat drew alongside, rowed by one woman.

'A Fin Wife! A Fin Wife!' they cried in terror.

'Ask her to sell us a wind,' suggested one bolder than the rest.

'If she comes aboard we are doomed and sunk!' muttered another.

While they argued, the woman sprang over the tafferel like a cat, and stood on deck. And Willie Norn started and stared, and cried,

'Annie, lass! Is this truly thee, Annie?'

'Oh ay!' says she. 'How's all the folk at home, Willie? Ay, lad, if blood were not thicker than water you had not seen me here this day.'

Then she turned to the crew.

'You great fools!' she cried. 'Why do you stand there gaping an' glowering at me as if I were a witch?'

And she bade them bring the vessel about, and took the helm herself, and called her orders as if she had been a born skipper. And when the ship got on the other tack, she made fine headway. In a little, the fog brightened ahead. Then it lifted, and the ship was lying in a land-locked bay calm as a lake. Beautiful hills and green valleys ran back from the shores all around. Many streams gushed sparkling down the hillsides, murmuring as they wimpled to the sea. Our Lady's hens, the skylarks, sang so loud that it seemed the very sky showered music down. This was part of Hilda-Land, the home of the Fin Folk above the waves, that is usually invisible to men. To the weary, storm-tossed sailors, it seemed a perfect haven.

Annie took the men on shore and led them up to a grand house, saying it was her home.

'By my faith, lass,' says Willie, her cousin, 'it's no wonder that you left Orkney, for you're well off here!'

'Oh, Willie,' says Annie, 'it's refreshing to hear an oath once more, for I never heard an oath or any swearing since I left my own human kind. No, no! Fin Folk don't spend their breath in swearing. And, boys, I tell you all, you had best not swear while in Hilda-Land! And mind well – while you are here, a close tongue keeps a safe head.'

Then she took the men into the big hall and gave them plenty of meat and drink. And then she showed them to beds, and they slept they did not know how long. When they awoke there was a great feast prepared for them. All the neighbouring Fin Men were bidden, and came riding on sea-horses.

Annie's goodman sat in the high seat and bade the mariners hearty welcome to Hilda-Land. When the feast was ended, Annie said to them that they should go on board the ship and make for home.

But the skipper said that he did not know which way to steer.

'Take no thought for that,' said his host. 'We will give you a pilot. His boat lies alongside your ship now. Each of you must throw a silver shilling into the boat as pilot's fee.'

Then they went down to the shore, Annie and Willie Norn walked behind, talking about old times. And many a kind message Annie sent to her own folk. Willie pressed her to come home with him, but she refused.

'No, no,' she said. 'I'm over well-off here to think of leaving. And tell my mother I have three bonnie bairns.'

Then she drew from her pocket a token tied to a string of otter's hair, and gave it to Willie.

'I know you were courting Mary Foubister, and she's not sure of taking you, for she has many offers. But when you get home, hang this token about her neck, and I warrant she'll like you better than any other.'

The men said farewell to Annie on the beach, and her husband rowed them to the ship. Each of the crew flung his silver shilling into the pilot's boat alongside. One dark-faced Fin Man sat in it, and as the silver fell, he laughed, for the Fin Men dearly love silver money. When they had all got on board and were to say farewell to Annie's husband, he says,

'O my good friends, I have long wished to see men playing at cards. Will ye play one game with me before sailing?'

'That we will, and welcome!' says the skipper. 'I have a pack in the locker below.'

So they all went below, dealt out, and began playing cards in the cabin. Now it may be that the parting-cup at the end of the Fin Men's feast was drugged, or it may be that the Fin Folk had wrought some of their spells, I do not know. But before the third trick was turned, every one of the Orkney crew sank into a heavy sleep, some lying with their heads on the table and some sprawled on the lockers. And there they slept and slept, none knew how long – it might have been hours or it might have been days.

The skipper was the first to wake. Rubbing his eyes, he ran up the ladder, and as he stuck his head out of the companionway, the first thing he clapped eyes on was the Crag of Gaitnup. He roused his men, and as they came on deck, they saw with joy that the vessel was anchored safe and snug in Scapa Bay, and the morning sun was glinting on the weather-cock of the spire of Saint Magnus. Were they not glad to be so near home!

Willie Norn hung the token he got from Annie around Mary Foubister's neck. And six weeks after that, they were married.

But fair Annie Norn was never seen or heard of more.

W.T.C.

Rest in Peace

When Robbie Swanson was fishing off Elsness this day, he thought he would look at his sheep on the holm. He pulled the boat into a little geo and stepped ashore. Several seals flopped into the water as he crossed the ebb. Two or three of his sheep were nibbling weed along the rocks; others lay up under the rough wall of a little ruin in the middle of the holm. Now but a shelter for the beasts, it was thought to have once been a Culdee priest's cell.

Wild as deer, the sheep scampered off as he approached. Then a large furry creature crouched under the wall moved and stood up. It was a woman in a long cloak of fine silver-grey sealskin fastened at the throat with a splendid silver clasp, a good-looking woman neither young nor old. Fair hair showed under the furry hood, her face was pale and unlined, her hands smooth, and wide silver bracelets gleamed on her wrists. But her eyes were strained and wild, and ever she looked from side to side like a hunted beast.

Robbie gazed at her in amazement.

'How came you here, goodwife?' he asked.

'Ask no questions,' she muttered. 'A close tongue keeps a safe head. They brought me here at dawn – take me away before the day ends . . .!'

'Where are you going?' demanded Robbie.

'To the kirkyard, if I am not dragged off first to hell!' she answered wildly. 'Take me away, man – my time is short – the sun is low. Take me away to the priest. I must

make my confession and hear the bonie-words before the sun sets . . .'

'Where did you come from ?'

'No matter,' replied the woman, looking nervously about her. 'Take me to the good land, and to the priest – I have siller,' she added urgently. 'Good siller!'

She thrust a coin at Robbie, and his hand shrank from her cold fingers. It was no coinage that he knew. 'It is siller!' she repeated, nodding, 'Good siller!'

The weight indeed was good, and Robbie, nodding in turn, dropped it into his pocket.

'Come, then, goodwife,' he said. 'The tide will turn soon.'

At the edge of the ebb, the woman halted. 'Carry me down,' she said. 'I dare not set foot in the ebb – I dare not!'

Robbie stared in surprise. She had, he realized now, a worn look; she was older too than he had thought.

'Come, goodwife,' he said gently, taking her by the arm. She drew back in terror.

'No! No!' she cried shrilly. '*Carry* me over! The black Nucklevee will bear me away for ever if I set foot in the ebb!'

A chill ran over Robbie and his skin prickled. But he had taken the silver, and a bargain's a bargain.

The poor soul is mad, he told himself. She was not very heavy and he easily carried her down over the ebb. And all the while she shook and shuddered like one in mortal terror. Once he had set her in the boat, however, she drew a deep breath and the wild look left her eye.

'O for the good land!' she murmured. 'And my long rest in the kirkyard with my own folk lying near!'

'Cheer up, goodwife!' said Robbie. 'You have time to spare before talking of the kirkyard.' He pushed off, giving the boat the usual turn to the right.

'A good lad!' said the woman, smiling strangely. 'Wi' thee I'll win through . . .'

Her voice trailed away into silence and she sat gazing towards the land. Robbie grasped his oars. Soon, above their faint splashing and the creak of the oarlocks, he heard a faint rustling and a mournful sighing. He stole a glance at his passenger, but she sat still as a stone. Her eyes were fixed on the land, her face drawn and sallow in the sunlight.

'What grieves you, goodwife?' he said at last. 'Such a sighing I never heard in this boat before.'

'No matter,' she said with a sideways look. 'It is the years passing over my head. Many a lifetime went by while mine stood still in Finfolkaheem – and now those years must pass over me before I die this day and be as other folk.'

She fell silent and Robbie knew beyond a doubt that he carried an uncanny passenger. He rowed harder with the doleful sighing ever in his ears.

'The flood's set in,' said Robbie at last. 'I can take you beyond that point into the bay and right up to the Lady Kirk. Will you feel safe there, goodwife?'

'Safe, aye, safe!' she cried. 'Safe from those de'ils . . .!'

Her voice had quavered oddly, and Robbie looked full at her. Again a chill fell on him, for in the last hour her face had hollowed into age and her hair was grey and wispy under the hood.

'Woman!' he cried hoarsely. 'What are you?'

'Flesh and bone like yourself, man,' she said in the same flat, cracked tones. 'Flesh and bone that have lasted long – too long – see how I dwindle . . .'

The hand she held out, smooth and firm an hour before, was shrunken now, veined and blotched with age. She drew it back under her cloak, and as in a dream Robbie saw that the garment itself had grown old and shabby. The silver bracelet slipped off the skinny wrist and tinkled down into the bottom of the boat, but she scarcely glanced at it.

'Fin Men's silver!' she muttered. 'That is past. I am coming to my rest – safe – safe – with my own human kind!'

The land neared: the green fields, smoke from a chimney, and up from the bay, the grey kirk. The sun was falling into the west.

'Here is the Lady Kirk, goodwife,' said Robbie.

'I must find the priest,' said the woman anxiously. Stiffly she moved on the thwart.

'No! No!' said Robbie. 'No priests these days – just the minister of the Scottish Kirk, good man.'

The old woman sank back with a bitter cry. 'O, who will hear me?' she wailed. 'Who will say an eerison for me and the bonie-words to send me to my grave in peace?'

'Who but the minister?' said Robbie. 'He is the man o' God – and there he is, coming down to the Kirk!'

He pulled in, got out of the boat and walked up to greet the minister, who was waiting for him.

'Good-day, Robbie,' he said. 'What brings you here at this time of day?'

'I've an old body aboard who must talk to you, Mr Tulloch. And I tell you fairly – she's a queer case!'

'Who is she?'

'Best only knows,' said Robbie with conviction. '*I* took her off the holm.'

'*Off the holm*? How did she get there?'

'In no canny way, I'll be bound. I'll bring her ashore.'

He was aghast at the change in his passenger even since he had been out of the boat. He lifted her out, light now as a sack of chaff, and carried her through the shallow water.

'You did not say she was as old as that,' muttered Mr Tulloch as he glimpsed the wrinkled face.

'Deed, Mr Tulloch, when I took her off the holm, she was no' this old, not by many years!' muttered Robbie, setting the ancient creature on her feet. She clung to his arm and he supported her, for she could no longer stand upright.

'What can I do for you, goodwife?' asked the minister.

'O, sir!' she said quaveringly. 'Hear me, and say an eerison for me. I have lived too long outside human kind. The Fin Folk stole me from the ebb long years ago, and I have lived their life in Hildaland, and when Hildaland was lost, in Finfolkaheem . . .'

The minister was wordless, but Robbie Swanson asked curiously, 'How do they live?'

'Much like folk above the water,' said the old woman, 'but far more easy, for their magic makes all things easy. And they feast in the bonny hall of Finfolkaheem. Its floor shines like the moon on the water and a rainbow holds up its roof and its walls are clear like glass. And the curtains over the doors are like the Merry Dancers. And O such lovely music and singing, and dancing in the great hall! But sirs! I tell you there is little joy in Finfolkaheem. For soon enough comes around the ninth feast and every ninth feast the black Nucklevee rides through the hall – and all the feast falls silent and the music dies away. And such a sight he is – black, black – a great black giant on a great black horse and all one fearsome beast, and his eyes flaming red. And one he takes every ninth feast – one to the black Nucklevee. He stops at that one's seat and that one mounts behind him and O his face is pale and his eyes staring like the eyes of the dead. He mounts and rides away – rides away to hell, for sirs – the black Nucklevee is the De'il's messenger in Finfolkaheem, and few that see him will escape . . .

'And whiles he takes a big Fin Man or a bonny Mermaid, and whiles a lass stolen like me from the ebb, or a brave lad caught from a sinking boat. And all must mount and go. Ever they think of that in Finfolkaheem, and there is little joy in that fair land. The ninth feast comes, and many empty seats are in that fine hall since first they took me from the ebb . . .'

The minister was the first to speak. 'How did you get on the holm?' he asked.

'O, sir, I never made my prayer to *him*, and when I sat at the feast, I thought always how the kirk and kirkyard looked in the sun, and always the Nucklevee passed me by. And always I asked to be taken home, and the Fin Folk laughed at me. "When iron floats" they said, and laughed, for they have hard, cold hearts. But today they set me on the holm, and told me to get to land as best I could, for the Nucklevee would fetch me at sunset. Tonight it is the ninth feast . . .'

'God help you, poor soul!' said Mr Tulloch.

'Well, Mr Tulloch, I suppose you could say that iron floated the other week when they launched that great iron ship,' said Robbie Swanson.

The minister nodded silently, but the woman uttered an eerie cry of joy.

'And the iron floated? Now the power of the Fin Folk is gone – now I am safe!' She turned to the minister.

'I will say my eerison and hear the bonie-words and join my own folk in the kirkyard. Now it comes back to me . . .'

She fell on her knees, murmuring 'Mary Moder . . .'

'No, no!' said the minister. 'We don't say that now. Say *"Our Father . . ."'*

The old woman caught her breath in a sob. 'O sir, it is long since *that* eerison passed my lips. I dared not say it in Finfolkaheem – *they* said it wrong.* I was feared to say it there.'

'Say it now, after me, and it will be right,' said Mr Tulloch.

'Our Father which art in heaven . . .'

'Our Father . . .' quavered the old voice hesitating, 'which *art* in – safe! Safe! Our Father which *art* in Heaven – Mary Moder –'

She toppled over in a little heap. When the two men raised the tattered, rotten sealskin cloak they saw a little pile of crumbling bones and a tarnished glint of ancient silver.

W.T.C.

---

* *They* would have said 'Our Father which *wert* in Heaven' – i.e. prayed to Satan.

ECHOES OF
THE SAGAS

St Magnus for Orkney

1. *The Invasion*

My father was up on Orphir's Ward Hill with three other watchers. Outside our cottage my mother and the other wives stood in the gloom of the very early morning gazing southwards. Suddenly the beacon on the Ward Hill of South Ronaldsay flared up, followed by that on Hoy's Ward. We looked up to our own Ward Hill, and it shot up a shower of sparks, and then flamed. Looking north and east we saw the beacons blaze on the Wards of every parish and island of the Orkneys – on Wideford, Fitty, Warsetter, and others.

'So they're left the Caithness shore,' a woman remarked. The invasion, expected for days, was coming.

Soon my father and his companions came running down the hillside. They passed us without a word, and went to the big house of Kirbister where all four worked. Then we heard a stamping as the men led out the horses. Kirbister himself appeared, big in his breastplate and steel helmet, sword girded to his side. With him came his steward with four Norse battle axes. These my father and his companions strapped to their backs.

We heard a clatter of hooves. Yarpha, the neighbouring udaller, and his four men rode up, armed as were those of Kirbister. Our men mounted, shouted farewells, and off they rode towards Kirkwall as the first light of dawn showed over the ridge of the Keelylang.

I turned as I heard Dick Budge's voice.

'The King's Army is out on the Pentland Firth, coming to punish the rebels,' he murmured. 'Our Earl of Caithness leads them on.'

'I hope a strong south-easter hurls them on the Pentland Skerries and lays them in smoosh,' I hissed. 'The Earl of Caithness has no right to come to Orkney.'

'The King of Scotland gave him the right,' Dick hissed back.

'The King of Scotland has no right either. The King of Norway is our right king.'

'Stop your yammering, boys, and be off to bed,' ordered my mother. 'You'll soon have to take the kye to the hill.'

She went into our cottage. The other women disappeared. We two boys stood in the half-darkness for a while.

'It's not worth going to bed now, Dick. Let's go to the hill slope and watch the beacons.

'All right, Harald, and we might see the King's Army coming over Scapa Flow.'

'Yes, and when we take the kye home at night we'll see the Orkneymen drive them back into the sea.'

Dick did not answer. We went up on the slope and watched one beacon after another die down, flicker, and disappear. As the last one went out we started arguing and quarrelling again. You see, Dick had come from Caithness two years back. His father had brought a load of sheep over to sell, and he put Dick into service as a herd boy with Yarpha. Dick was thirteen, and I was twelve. I liked him fine. Though we quarrelled, he never lifted a hand to me. But this invasion led by Lord Sinclair, the Earl of Caithness had divided us, for it was to take the two Sinclairs of Warsetter prisoners, because they had led the attack on Kirkwall Castle, and driven their cousin, Lord William Sinclair, from Orkney. All the Orkney udallers were with the Sinclair brothers, for Lord William was a bad one, and had squeezed rents and skats out of Orkneymen worse than the worst Norse Jarl.

Dick and I argued until it was time for us to go down and take the cattle of Kirbister and Yarpha out to the hill grazing ground. We each got our breakfast, Dick at Yarpha and I at Kirbister, took our sticks and drove the kye out over the rutted road, past the earthen treb dykes, and north to the far hill slope. When the cattle were all grazing, we came together, lay on the heath, and looked out over Scapa Flow, the waters bathed by light from the big red sun.

Near the Orphir shore, a thread of peat smoke rose from the stone chimney of Kirsty Gorn's thatched cottage. She was a Spae-Wife – one that knows what's going to happen. Folks said she never slept at night, but kept thinking up spells to find out what was going to be in the next day, or the next week, or the next month. She never bothered folks as the witches did, for she was a wise woman. I shivered as a chill morning breeze blew in from the sea. Dick rose, muttering that the Caithness boats should now be in sight.

'I hope our men get here in time to stop them landing,' I said as I rose. 'Don't you, Dick? You told me you were much better at Yarpha than at home with your father.'

'Better fed and clothed, and never beaten in two years. But you don't understand that I'm Caithness, and I know our earl will beat the island beardies and hang the two Sinclairs of Warsetter.'

'Island beardies!' I cried. 'They'll drive the miserable Scotch ferry-loupers back across the Pentland, and you with them.'

'Don't you see that this is the King's Army coming? It's not right to go against the King.'

'Him! James the Fifth was never our king. His grandfather got leave to take the rents and skats of Orkney for the Maid of Norway's dowry. She died there in South Ronaldsay, and she never married him, and he went and took all Orkney.'

'The dowry was pledged. A promise is a . . . Look, Harald, the boats of the King, and my earl leads them on.'

I looked, and over the Flow came the sails of fifty boats or more, faster than the light breeze could sail them. And a single skiff under full sail and rowed by six oars scudded east to Scapa, an Orkney boat going to warn the udallers at Kirkwall.

'Oh, Dick,' I cried, 'our men will never get here in time.'

'No, that's what comes of going against the King.'

'King!' I exclaimed, and spat.

'King James. My king.'

I was angry, for I saw Dick, his eyes bright and a smile on his face, watching that fleet coming louping over the ferry. At last he spoke.

'Let's go down to the shore, Harald, and see the great earl. The kye are all right here until evening. They won't bother about two herd boys.'

'Them! They're savages, and will kill every living thing they meet.'

'They won't, for I'm Caithness. Stay here then if you're frightened, poor island beardy.'

He set off, and I watched him for a distance. Then, stung by the thought that a Caithness boy was not frightened and I was, I ran after him and caught him up.

'Got over your fright, Harald?'

'I'm not frightened, no more than you.'

He did not answer. By the time we neared the shore, the first men had landed, and others were wading through the surf to the shore. Some were armed like our masters, some like my father, and others in checkered plaid and trews with big broadswords at their sides. We came to Kirsty Gorn's cottage. The Spae-Wife stood outside, a small woman, grey and wrinkled, clad in dark coak and kirtle. She held a ball of white wool in her left hand and one of black in her right. We stood near her, watching a big man in splendid armour approach, with a small man, and behind them men led two horses.

'The Earl,' breathed Dick.

The two leaders halted by the cottage, and the earl came forward, a huge savage-looking Highlander with him.

'Well, mother,' said the earl with a laugh. 'Read me your spell!'

Kirsty Gorn spoke no word for a moment. Then, looking up at the earl, she held out both hands, the ends of the wool hanging loose.

'Choose, my lord,' she said in a low voice. 'One ball will be yours, the other Orkney. The longer will be the winner.' The earl looked carelessly from one to the other of the balls, and took hold of the end of the white. Kirsty took it from him, put the end of the black even with it, and began winding both strands. She wound and wound, till the earl's ball dwindled and came to an end.

'So Orkney is to win,' said the earl lightly. 'That's a poor spell you give me, mother.'

'Not me, my lord. Fate. But I'll tell you one more. He on whose side the first blood is shed shall be the loser.'

Kirsty had no sooner finished than the big Highlander swung aloft his broadsword. Kirsty screamed 'Stop', but the blade flashed down splitting Dick's head. He fell all covered with blood and brains. I rushed into Kirsty s cottage, cowering in a corner, spattered with Dick's blood. I heard Kirsty say, 'A black deed, my lord. That lad is Caithness born.'

A muttering followed. Then the slow tramp of feet moving past the cottage, many feet going slowly inland. When the last man passed, Kirsty came in and saw me, and I sobbed in the corner.

'Stay here, Harald. They'll soon be gone. Then back to your kye, for tonight you must pen two herds. Poor Dick Budge.'

I stayed for an hour, still horrified even after Kirsty gave me hot broth. When I had drunk it, she said, 'Now, begone. Have no fear. They'll not kill another herd. Beaten men with no stomach for the battle! Poor Dick Budge. Holy St Magnus, help thou our Orkney!'

2   The Battle

The sky had darkened, the red sun of dawn no longer showing itself. Slowly I made my way back to the eastern slope of Ward Hill where we had left the herds. They had wandered north, far away to the Mid Hill, where I found them on a slope above the ridge of the valley of Summerdale. Below this ridge there was a confused mass of struggling men in the boggy ground. I could not make out who were the Orkneymen and who were the Scottish soldiers. Soon, however, many men, no longer carrying their arms fled over the slope, running to the shore where they had left their boats, all of them invaders. More and more followed, and then came the udallers, slaughtering those who stood and fought with their axes, and rounding up those who threw down their arms. There was no sign of the earl on his charger.

The defeated fled beneath me, the herds began to bellow, and run with their tails up, higher on the hill. I could do nothing to stop them, and did not try, for they were safe up there.

A lighting of the southern sky made me turn and look. A beam of sunshine shot round the brow of the Ward, and lit a patch in the dark sky. The patch moved and swirled up and down. I wondered if a rainbow was appearing, but told myself there had been no rain. The patch stopped moving, and grew in size. In shape it looked like a large kneeling figure, a rough cross over the head.

I heard a shout from the valley: 'St Magnus! St Magnus for Orkney.'

I stared hard at the patch. For a moment it did look like the image of the saint that I had seen in the kirk, and then it grew dim and faded. 'St Magnus! St Magnus!' again rolled up the hillside. Could it have been him appearing? Kirsty had called him.

The rout swept past me, the fleeing having thrown away their arms. Now there was no fighting, those overtaken having laid down their arms and surrendered. The Orkneymen drove forward to the boats. The foremost of the fliers had already scrambled into the boats and put off not waiting for their comrades who, in reaching the shore dashed into the sea and hauled themselves into other boats, and put off. Then the udallers got between the shore and the foe, and there came an end to the pursuit as the remaining defeated laid down their weapons.

As evening drew on, I could see long lines of men, some on ponies, take the shore road to Kirkwall, the victors with their prisoners. To the north some men were going off eastward. These I thought would be our men taking the first men to surrender to Kirkwall. As they disappeared, I realized I had two herds to look after.

The cattle were quite ready to go home for the night, after their fright from the clashes in the valley. I herded them homeward. Four times one or two snorted, backed into the others, and ran round the bodies of men slashed by sword or axe. On the slope to Kirbister the herds moved quickly, my herd going straight into their enclosure, glad to get there, and the herd that had been Dick's care going on to Yarpha. I had no trouble penning them up for the night. Slowly I went to our cottage. No joy surged in me because of the Orkney victory. My father rode up to say he must go to Kirkwall, and trotted off.

Only the butchering of Dick Budge lay like a weight on my breast. His blood had dried in dark spots all over my clothing. I dragged my way into our cottage, and brokenly told my story at my mother's knee.

W.T.C.

The Procession

On the fifteenth of December, 1913, two boys of the Kirkwall Grammar School left the public library at closing time, and started walking up King Street. One walked with a limp; he was sixteen-year-old David Thomson, son of a lighthouse keeper, who had lodgings in the town. The other, Andrew Slater, was a year older, and lived in Kirkwall with his parents. They left King Street for the lane that ran along the east wall of St Magnus Cathedral grounds. The night was blustery and cold, a pale round moon passed behind one racing black cloud after another. They stopped, and craned over the wall to watch the shadows flee over the far headstones, and up over spire, tower, and cleristory. The moon went behind a cloud, and the boys continued up the lane to Palace Road.

'A ghostly night,' muttered David.

'It's going to snow, and some flurries will look ghostly,' said Andrew.

At Palace Road they stood for a minute before parting.

'There it comes,' exclaimed Andrew, as a flurry of sleet came whirling up Palace Road. 'Goodnight, David, and don't mistake snow flurries for ghosts!'

'Goodnight, Andrew. I'm not likely to make that mistake.'

Andrew walked with the wind, up towards his home. David, whose lodgings were in Clay Loan, faced the sleet as he walked along towards the Watergate and the Bishop's Palace. The sleet turned to heavy snow, clogging his eyes and nostrils. He came to a niche in the Cathedral wall, near the south gate, and pressed into it out of breath. Wiping the snow off his face, he decided to take shelter until the heavy snow eased off. The half-hour, 11.30, rang out, from the Cathedral tower. As the three-quarters sounded, the snow thinned to a few flakes, the wind died down, and the moon shone again.

Just as he was about to leave, a faint sound as of singing came to his ears. Who could be singing so late at night? Nearer and nearer came the sound. It was no group of drunk men, for it was a high-toned chant coming from the south door of the great church. David listened. Latin words, he realized, as the chant neared the gate. In wonder and dread the boy pressed hard into the niche as faint yellow lights flickered through the gate.

Black-stoled figures, each carrying a short thick candle, filed through and across the road to the Moosie Tower, as the tower on the Bishop's Palace was known locally. But now David could see neither the tower nor the ruins as he knew them. In its place stood a complete long two-storey building, roughly built and roofed in. Through the small windows at the far end yellow light shone. Eight black-clad figures crossed the road, followed by the crozier, and behind him a large man in dark embroidered robes – the bishop, David concluded. Weird shadows fell on the snow, cast by the guttering candles and not by the clear moonlight. Why did the monks' shadows not show? When the procession had crossed the road, the boy, his curiosity overcoming all fears, followed on slowly, accompanied by his own shadow now falling sharply on the wall of the strange hall. The monks filed through a side door, each taper disappearing. When the Bishop had entered, David slowly came to the door, where he stood looking and listening.

The chant sounded down from a spiral stairway up which the procession was winding. David knocked the snow off his boots, shook it off his clothes, and went in through the heavy wooden door to a room dimly lit by the light from two tall tapers. To his left was the foot of a stairway leading up into darkness overhead.

At each side of it stood a rigid figure clad in a short skin coat with steel rings attached, trousers thonged from thigh to shoe of hide. a steel helmet on his head. In their right hands, the sentries held long battle axes, the handles ending in spear points, the heads on the floor. They did not lift their heads as David entered. The boy stood fearful and uncertain, absent-mindedly drawing the library book he had borrowed from under his coat.

A monk, hurrying down the stairs, stopped when he saw David.

'Ha, page, what book have you brought to read to the King?'

'This,' stammered David, 'is the saga of Sverri and . . .'

'The King calls for it,' cried the monk. 'Follow me.'

David, in trepidation, followed up the spiral stairway to a panelled room with religious pictures painted on the walls. The monks were drawn up, four at each side, by a couch at the far end, their candles burning. At the head of the couch the Bishop was standing, and on it reclined an aged and emaciated figure clad in red and purple robes. The nose, like the beak of an eagle, stood out from sunken and ashen cheeks, the eyes watery blue, the long brow wrinkled, the eyebrows and the hair snow-white. The Bishop signalled David to approach.

'My page,' came in weak tones from the King, 'read me the saga of my grandfather, Sverri.'

Hurriedly David opened the book and began reading, his voice faltering at first, but gaining in strength and rhythm as his mind took in the saga, and as his eyes followed closely the lines. He paused at the end of a verse to glance at the King. The dull eyes now flashed steel-blue from flaxen lids, the brow rose smooth above the hooked nose. The Viking King! He half rose, but sank with a groan, his breathing loud and laboured.

'Quick, Brothers, bring the holy oil. Boy, be gone,' ordered the Bishop.

David hurried to the stairway, shutting his book, and down the stairs he stumbled, fearing he would break into sobs. He did not stop for the sentries, but went out into the snow to hear the last stroke of midnight ring out. His mind full of the dying King, he went back to his niche in the wall in order to watch the monks returning. With his eyes on the snow, he recalled the room, the monks, and the figure on the couch as they had appeared to him. The quarter past midnight rang out. The King would be dead now, holy unction having been administered.

No monks returned. There were no lights in the Bishop's Palace when David looked up. The Moosie Tower and the Palace as he knew them stood as they had stood after being rebuilt three hundred years after the death of Hakon Hakonson, grandson of Sverri, but in ruins. The flickering gas jet at the corner of Palace Road and Broad Street gave the only light he could see, apart from the moon, now casting long shadows on the green east of the Palace. David wondered if he had slept on his feet, and had one of his many vivid dreams. Had he really left this niche? But there were his own tracks in the snow, the uneven length of step; and no tracks of monks. He traced his steps to the southern doorway, through which he had followed the monks. Inside there was nothing but darkness, and a deep silence not even broken by the squeak of a mouse.

Slowly he wandered back to his lodgings. He looked up the Orkney Almanac for December. There it was.

December 15 King Hakon Hakonson, last of the great Norse sea-kings died in the Bishop's Palace at midnight 1263.

That was six hundred and fifty years ago.

But what of the tracks and the shadows. Of course! His tracks and shadow in his time and not in theirs. Their tracks and shadows in their time and not in his. Yet, somehow, between the striking of the Cathedral clock at 11.45 and midnight the two times had crossed and recrossed.

W.T.C.